Hopeless

Lesley Choyce

author of

In The Kingdom of Cheese
There Are No Heroes

Hopeless
© 2025 Lesley Choyce

Cover design: Rebekah Wetmore
Editor: Andrew Wetmore

ISBN: 978-1-998149-96-4
First edition October, 2025

Moose House Publications
2475 Perotte Road, Annapolis County, NS B0S 1A0
moosehousepress.com / info@moosehousepress.com

Moose House Publications recognizes the support of the Province of Nova Scotia. We are pleased to work in partnership with the Department of Communities, Culture and Heritage to develop and promote our cultural resources for all Nova Scotians.

We live and work in Mi'kma'ki, the ancestral and unceded territory of the Mi'kmaw people. This territory is covered by the "Treaties of Peace and Friendship" which Mi'kmaw and Wolastoqiyik (Maliseet) people first signed with the British Crown in 1725. The treaties did not deal with surrender of lands and resources but in fact recognized Mi'kmaq and Wolastoqiyik (Maliseet) title and established the rules for what was to be an ongoing relationship between nations. We are all Treaty people.

Also by Lesley Choyce

Accro d'la Planche
All Alone at the End of the World
An Avalanche of Ocean
Around England with a Dog
Beautiful Sadness
Big Burn
Billy Botzweiler's Last Dance
The Book of Michael
Breaking Point
Broken Man on a Halifax Pier
Carrie's Crowd
Carrie's Camping Adventure
Carrie Loses Her Nerve
Caution to the Wind
Clearcut Danger
Climbing Knocknarea
Closing Down Heaven
The Coasts of Canada
The Coastline of Forgetting
Cold Clear Morning
Couleurs Troubles
Coming Up for Air
Conventional Emotions
Crash
Dance The Rocks Ashore
Dark End of Dream Street
December Six/The Halifax Solution
Deconstructing Dylan
Den Jag Ar
The Discipline of Ice

Downwind
The Dream Auditor
Driving Minnie's Piano
Dumb Luck
Eastern Sure
Ecstasy Conspiracy
Edible Wild Plants of the Maritimes
The End of Ice
The End of the World as We Know It
Face the Music
Falling Through the Cracks
Famous At Last
Fast Living
Far Enough Island
Full Tilt
Gone Bad
Go For It Carrie
Good Idea Gone Bad
Hell's Hotel
How to Fix Your Head
Hungry Lizards
Identify
I'm Alive. I Believe in Everything
In Praise of Small Mistakes
In the Kingdom of Cheese There Are No Heroes
Into the Wasteland
Jeremy Stone
Konec Skrivalnic
Krytponite

...continued next page

Last Chance
Living Outside the Lines
Los Pandemonium
Magnificent Obsessions
*The Man Who Borrowed the
    Bay of Fundy*
Margin of Error
Never the Same Sea Twice
Nova Scotia: Shaped By the Sea
Off the Grid
*Peggy's Cove: the Amazing
    History of a Coastal Village*
Plank's Law
Random
Raising Orion
Rat
Reaction
Reckless
Refuge Cove
Re-Inventing the Wheel
The Republic of Nothing
Revenge of the Optimist
Rock
Roid Rage
The Rules Have Changed
Running the Risk
Saltwater Chronicles
Scam
Sea of Tranquility

*The Second Season of Jonas
    MacPherson*
Seven Ravens
Shoulder the Sky
Sid the Kid and the Dryer
Skateboard Shakedown
Skate Freak
Skatefreaks Og Graesrodder
Skunks for Breakfast
Smoke and Mirrors
Some Kind of Hero
Sudden Impact
The Ledge
The Summer of Apartment X
The Thing You're Good At
The Top of the Heart
*The Unlikely Redemption of
    John Alexander MacNeil*
*The Untimely Resurrection of
    John Alexander MacNeil*
Thin Places
Transcendental Anarchy
The Trap Door To Heaven
Thunderbowl
Typographical Eras
Wave Warrior
Wavewatch
World Enough
Wrong Time, Wrong Place

In memory of Sharon Green Moul

This is a work of fiction. The author has created the characters, conversations, interactions, and events; and any resemblance of any character to any real person is coincidental.

Hopeless

Hopeless

Lesley Choyce

1

My father coined the nickname for me. Hopeless. And it stuck.

"This one's hopeless," he must have said to my mother when I was very very young. "Really, truly hopeless."

I can't remember this, of course, but my mother has remembered it for me. Many times.

I'm guessing it was because I was refusing to be toilet trained. And other things as well. They said I was stubborn from the day I was born, or even before I was born. Apparently, I did not want to leave the womb. Perhaps I didn't want to get born at all. Some of us are like that, you know.

I mean, think about it. Seriously think about it. If you sum up all the crappy stuff you have to do in life—squeeze out into the bright cold world, cry yourself to sleep each night, figure out how to poop and pee into a toilet, etc., etc....And it just keeps getting crappier and more complicated after that.

If only I could reverse engineer myself back into oblivion. That's what I think would be nice. Well, sometimes I think that. I really do.

So you can call me Hopeless, too, if you like.

And then, you might wonder, if it's all so hopeless, why is

he bothering to write this all down? I mean, is he going to be taking us right back to the womb and the potty chair even before the story gets going? Do we need to know all that?

Well, it's just a warm-up, see, for the story I am obliged to write if I want to get through school and go out into the larger, even colder and brighter, world.

If you're reading this, I want you to know that I'm not writing it because I was inspired or consider myself a writer. Truth was, I was threatened. My teacher, Mr. Tasker, gave me an ultimatum. He held off on calling me hopeless for quite a long time. Then gave in to the reality of it all.

(Reality, there's a topic to get me going. Reality so often conflicts with my ideal life that I sometimes find it annoying, if not downright insulting.)

You see, I disappeared from school towards the end of the academic year, and he thought that was it, that I had finally given up. He probably tried calling my mom, but she'd not paid her cell phone bill for several months and it had been cut off.

Then, when I suddenly showed up and told him I didn't want to talk about what I had been doing, he got really mad. And he, too, was ready to give up on me, the ultimate helpless one. The one who couldn't be helped.

As it turned out, Mr. Tasker was my unflagging taskmaster, my intended guru, my mind-numbing mental mentor, my would-be academic saviour, my educational super-supervisor, my relentless pestering pedagogue. Yes, him. He had tried everything under the sun to get me to do work, and it was like toilet training all over again. I pointed this out to him. And still he did not give up. (His reality, as you can imagine, is much different than mine.)

But bear with me on this until I get to the point. I need first to explain my educational career—or my lack thereof.

Me and school—school and myself—the educational prison of our contemporary society and this free-thinking hopeless one—we never got along. Ever.

When I was younger, I liked to throw things. (Actually, I still like to throw things.) As I grew older, it was revealed to anyone within earshot that I was as stubborn as a rusty nail, as my own grandfather said.

His name was Grant. Grandfather Grant. He tried to take credit for my stubborn habits. "He's inherited the stubborn gene from me," he liked to say. "My own great grandfather brought it over on the boat from Ireland. He comes by it honestly." The stubbornness, he meant.

But more on all this later—my youth, my ineptitude in the pedagogical arena, etc. etc.

I am writing this, I remind you, because everyone in the educational system gave up on me except Tasker. When I told him about the stubborn gene coming over on the boat from Ireland with my great grandfather, he smiled. He said that he was pretty sure his own great-great-great grandfather was on that boat, with what he called the *perseverance* gene.

I don't know why, but I countered that with an insult. Somewhere along the way, I had inadvertently learned something about deductive reasoning. I explained to Mr. Tasker that it is a known fact that all teachers suck and that Mr. Tasker himself is obviously a teacher (tsk, tsk). Thus, (ipso facto) Tasker must suck.

When I said this to him, he just smiled. That damn perseverance gene up against my stubborn gene again.

Long-winded, you say. The boy is not only dense, but he is long-winded, wordy and, as Tasker points out, if I'm so verbose, so pseudo-intellectual, using big words and long, convoluted sentences, then why the frig (his word) don't I just do the work, breeze through school and allow it to vomit me out into the bright, blue world as an adult?

Why?

Because.

So, let's just say that the traditional educational system we call public school failed me. And I failed it. The feelings were mutual. In fact, we failed each other over and over for a good decade. A lot of energy was wasted. A lot of blocks and books and desks were thrown. Several (six, I think) well-meaning educators took me on as a special case.

And I defeated those well-meaning and, in their own way, hopeless individuals who falsely believed in the essential good of all members of the human race. I almost came through it all with my dignity intact and my hopelessness thoroughly affirmed by highly educated men and women with teachers' credentials, master's degrees, doctoral degrees and post-doctoral degrees.

And then, after the system, the bloody educational system, was about to give up on me and throw me to the wolves, Tasker came along.

So, to get to the point, and I believe I do have a point, Tasker said this: "Hopeless, you can tell me to fuck off as many times as you like." And I already had taken upon myself to fulfill this request. "And you can throw tantrums or tires or tin cups or tirades." Well, mostly tantrums and tirades. "But I'm going to see this through."

Now *there* was a challenge. Like they used to say in the old days, he threw down the gauntlet. In case you are not familiar, a gauntlet was a glove made of steel that soldiers once wore with a suit of armour. If you "threw down the gauntlet" that was a symbol of challenge.

And then finally this.

"Write me your story," he literally snarled. "Write about you and the world around you as you see it. Write the definitive story of you. Do it reasonably well, and I'll find a way to grant you a high school diploma."

"Define definitive," I countered, because I always countered everything a teacher ever said to me.

"Serving to define precisely. Authoritative and exhaustive."

"Exhaustive? Really?"

"Well, 50,000 words' worth."

"50,000?" That sounded like a lot of words.

"Not a word less. And you bloody well better include writing about where you've been these last few weeks when you weren't in school. And if you can include what happened to that morose brother of yours who seems to have disappeared from his last weeks of senior year, that might help."

I thought about it, but only for a few seconds, because I thought Tasker was going to blow a gasket. The man looked frustrated to the point that he was going to explode.

"Deal," I finally said.

But I didn't mean it. I was just playing him along.

"Then do it, dammit."

So I took out a sheet of paper and wrote him down one word: *Hopeless*. I even added an illustration to emphasize the point. "I don't need 50,000 words, sir. This pretty well sums it up."

I held it up to his face—right up to his oh-so-unfashionable glasses. Smushed it right up there.

And you know what he did? The fucker just smiled.

"Perfect," he said with what I might call an elfin grin. "Now give me 49,999 more words and you're home free."

And with that, he turned and walked away.

49,999 words, I thought. *My* story in all its inglorious miserable details. No one had ever really understood me, and I was certain no one ever would. So I was sure I would be wasting my time.

But *fuck it*, I thought. I'd write him some bullshit thing and take the deal.

I wasn't sure I was ready to talk about what had happened during the recent time Garrett and I had been away from school. I wasn't sure anyone, even Tasker, would understand. But I already had that one word. And no, it wouldn't be the first word of my story, as you can see. I'd save it and put it at the end of the first chapter just to reinforce all the points I had just made.

Hopeless.

2

You are reading this because Tasker said he would get the damn thing published, even if just on the internet…if I hit my quota of 50,000 words.

So the stubborn Irish gene handed down to me by my great-grandfather Grant believed that maybe I could just sit down and write that first word over and over. Or just figure out a way for the word processor program to repeat it 49,999 times or more. Cut and paste. Cut and paste for a morning and an afternoon.

But.

After staring off into space for nearly twenty minutes, it occurred to me I had a story.

A story worth telling.

Perhaps the worthless story of a hopeless boy. But still, it was a story.

I thought I'd simply riff on the theme of being the crown prince of hopelessness, but when I looked up words that equated to hopeless, I found synonyms like *despondent, downhearted, depressed, miserable, forlorn* and even *pathetic, inept, clueless, terrible*. None of them felt quite right.

So I decided to dip into my past the way those dipshit psychiatrists had tried to get me to do over the years. The ones hired by the school board for delinquents like me.

As previously noted, it was my father, apparently, who labelled me hopeless first. He was, no doubt, comparing me to my older brother, Garrett, who will be central to this story.

I don't remember much about my father from when I was young because he left us soon after my mother's attempts to toilet-train me. He told my mother he couldn't handle family life anymore, and so he left.

What he really meant was that he couldn't handle me. So he opted to be a delinquent father, a proverbial deadbeat dad.

I wish I had at least one good thing to say about him, but I don't. If I had known him better, I probably would say it wasn't much of a loss. But my mother now had her hands full.

Garrett was no problem. My mom referred to him as her "golden boy." This is often a painful thorn for the younger, lesser sibling like me. Any of you who have had glorified older brothers or sisters understand what this does to a little raucous tyke such as I was.

Mom did her best to support Garrett and to tame me, and she did a serviceable job. Well, Garrett could handle just about anything on his own from an early age. He skipped ahead a grade at school while I was being left back.

But I don't think he ever once called me hopeless or pathetic, or inept, or even clueless. My mother used the word "terrible", though, on many occasions, and he picked it up sometimes. Who could blame him?

But I can see now that this story has an awful lot to do

with Garrett as well as me, because of the way things turned out. So I probably need to skip ahead and leave out the boring parts so that I can share an adventure—or misadventure, as Tasker would say. This will set things up nicely for the unexpected events that followed.

Now, I don't know about your life. But my life really doesn't have a coherent plotline. What it does have is a series of disjointed stories that make up a narrative. And Tasker kept insisting I needed to stay focused on what he called "anecdotes" from my life and "pivotal experiences" that somehow, he alleged, shaped me.

So I guess I should jump to the story about the ice. If you live some place warm where there is no ice, you'll probably think I made this up. But I did not.

Garrett the golden boy believed that life really was an adventure, and he did his best to bolster my inept life of nothingness into something better. But, in the long run, it didn't turn out as planned.

3

Although we grew up in Halifax, just a stone's throw from the Northwest Arm, I never really enjoyed swimming, and my mother didn't believe that we should take up sailing small dinghies around the Arm like so many of the other snotty kids in the neighbourhood.

Garrett was an outward boy. Outward bound, often bounding out of the house to go running or hiking through the woods at Point Pleasant Park or riding his bicycle through the Armdale Roundabout and out to Herring Cove. By the age of fifteen he was, of course, free to go wherever he wanted to go.

I was only twelve and always wanted to tag along, but only could when Garrett decided it was safe. My mom let him make a lot of decisions about what I could do and couldn't do.

And I know I must have been a real albatross around his neck, but if he thought it was safe, he'd let me play sidekick. I'm sure I didn't show it because that was never my style, but I truly appreciated his acceptance.

Whenever my mom berated me for being such a hopeless little weasel, Garrett would take me aside and say something like, "Nick, the truth is you are a hopeless little weasel, but you're *my* hopeless little weasel of a brother and you're still young. You'll grow out of it, just like that blue snowsuit that doesn't fit you anymore."

But it wasn't like the snowsuit at all.

My mother had become obsessed with feeding us "whole foods," but was victim to the whole Kellogg/Kraft/Betty Crocker conspiracy that kept us eating highly-processed foods that simply claimed to be healthy. She eventually kicked that commercial habit once she fell in with a posse of Buddhist vegans from Colorado who set her straight. After that, there was no more Quaker granola, only some bland-as-dust organic fare hand-picked and prepared by some hippies in the Annapolis Valley.

But when not meditating or reading books on whole foods and preparing exotic vegetarian dishes with something called jack fruit, she was urging both of us to become free spirits and spend as much time outdoors as possible.

The "out of doors," as my mother called it, did not particularly inspire me, and, besides, that was Garrett's domain. Yet he did take me along at random times to Point Pleasant Park or down by the Arm near the Roundabout where people docked their dories and rowboats and canoes. We'd skip flat stones across the blue water on warm days in the summer until a cold fog slipped in from the Atlantic or a group of local bully-types showed up to wreck our fun.

Garrett had a way with bullies that, if studied, no doubt could have been replicated and saved generations of young victims from suffering through their adolescence. I didn't have to do much myself, thanks to my older brother.

Bully A would show up with at least three henchmen—

observers who sneered at me and seemed to be along just to be able to report back to other wannabee bullies. Then Bully A would taunt me with obscenities and, at the appropriately timed moment, would shove me hard on the shoulder so I would topple over on the sharp stones beneath my feet.

If I was alone, that was pretty much the whole story and, with a little embellishment, the tale would have garnered a good guffaw from whatever young louts hung out with these assholes. But if Garrett was there, things went differently.

The taunt would be delivered on schedule, the stone skipping would cease, and Garrett would look the bully in the eye, smile, amble over to him (with the other young louts drooling for a fight perhaps) and say something like, "You look like you'd be a good runner. Wanna run with me sometime? I'm trying to work up to a marathon, but I'm not quite there yet. How about we do five K tomorrow morning at six?"

I always, always expected the young hulk (who looked like a slob, not a runner) to tell Garrett to fuck off, but he (whoever the latest *he* was) never did. Sometimes the goon would answer, "Maybe," a little self-consciously and that was that. Or sometimes the goon was so at a loss for words that he didn't lose the attitude but didn't want to hang around anyway and he'd say something to his cronies like, "Let's get the fuck away from these assholes and go do something more important."

I always wanted to ask the lad what could possibly be more important than harassing a twelve-year-old and his fifteen-year-old brother on a fine, clear day. But I always knew enough to keep my mouth shut. In fact, at moments like that I strangely *liked* to keep my mouth shut. Which was something I hardly ever did unless I was in Garrett's presence.

Garrett was this big, bright, shining sun in my life and sometimes I loved him for it and sometimes I hated him for it. But I'd probably have not lived to tell this tale had he not been my protector.

And I don't mean just the bullies. Point Pleasant Park's adolescent bullies were tame compared to some of the tyrants I encountered at school.

But this is not a story about bullies, since that one has been told over and over, relentlessly, since the invention of language, and such intimidators will not go away with the passage of time. Let me get to the real story.

It goes like this.

We were down at the Arm on a brisk day in February, that winter when I was still twelve. It was clear and windless, but the water was all jammed up with sheets of pack ice—slob ice or junk ice, as I heard some call it. Some of it was piled up near the shore and it was great fun to jump on a big slab or two and crash down as it broke off with us on it.

Garrett, however, got bored with that and said he needed to burn off some energy. "I'm gonna run to the Roundabout and once around the Walmart parking lot and be back in fifteen minutes. I just need to clear some of those cobwebs out of my brain."

"Sure," I said. "I'll just wait for you here."

I kind of wished I could have done the same to my brain. I didn't have cobwebs so much as dark, heavy clouds in my head, clouds so dark and dense that the sun could never burn them away.

But here was a sunny, clear, winter day at the Arm, and off my brother ran like a young antelope. I studied the water dripping from the ice pans in the morning sunlight and thought it looked quite beautiful, which is so unlike me. But it had me transfixed.

I soon got bored, however, and began walking across the large ice pans near the shoreline, the grounded ones at first. Then I leaped to my first floaty one. And then another.

I was cautious, okay? I only picked the bigger, more solid ones and found myself jumping—no, leaping—from one to the next. Each one seemed as solid as the last one and I thought how cool it would be for Garrett to return from his running foray to see his little brother bounding from ice island to ice island.

And I guess I would have remained on a sensible course parallel to shore had I not spotted some kind of derelict low-lying boat—a skiff, I guess you'd call it, a small, low, flat-bottomed, snub-nosed aluminum boat that was tucked behind one of the larger pans of floating ice.

I angled over to it and peered down at the couple of inches of ice in the bottom. There was a compass frozen in there, something that looked really old and historic, and I couldn't help but crabwalk my way off the ice into the little craft to try to chip it out with my shoe.

I hadn't been paying attention at all to the fact that the wind had come up out of the north. I sat in the little boat, feeling like the king of the white glistening wonderland of winter.

I couldn't crack the ice on the floor and was giving up on the compass altogether when I suddenly noticed that I was no longer just surrounded by white ice but also by open blue water. The ice pans, driven by the rising north wind, were being pushed out to sea and the skiff, with mortal me in it, was jammed between two big ice pans.

Some people react quickly in such situations and extricate themselves with powerful instincts to get themselves to safety. I was not one of those people. I was somewhat shocked at first by how quickly this had happened. Fascinated, really. But immobile. Brain-frozen, stupefied, incredulous, dumbfounded and paralyzed.

This can't be happening, my befuddled brain insisted. *This can't be a happening to me.*

But it was.

I saw no one on the shore anywhere, so logic told me it would be useless to yell. I know. Anyone else would have yelled anyway. But not me.

As the wind continued to rise, the ice continued to move southward towards the open Atlantic with me in the stupid little skiff sitting upright, appalled and amazed at once with a rising tide of fear far back in the nether regions of my skull. I looked down at the compass still frozen in the clear ice on the floor as if asking it for advice. It had little to offer.

I looked out to sea. I studied the armada of ice that had me locked into its formation. And I suddenly realized how wet and cold I was. I wondered if this was how I was going to die.

The water was getting choppy now as the ice pans began tilting up and down. It would not be long before the boat would be swamped, and me with it.

I looked back towards the small park where we had been fooling around on the shore. And there I saw my brother, running along the shoreline now. He had obviously seen my predicament and was running as hard as he could, but he was soon halted by a fence.

I saw him throw his hands up in the air and yell something at me, words that were immediately stolen by the wind.

4

What happened next, I think really happened, but it felt more like a dream. Garrett took to the shifting ice, leaping from one pan to the next, fighting his way in my direction. He was more clown-like than graceful, but he was making progress.

I yelled something to him—syllables, not words—and they, too, were swallowed by the wind. I foolishly dipped my hands in the water, thinking I could somehow use them to slow my progress and maybe paddle towards my brother. But it was useless. My hands immediately began to burn from the cold, and I almost instantly lost the feeling in my fingers.

My eyes were riveted on my running, leaping brother. He had to zig and zag to make progress and I watched as he slipped into the water more than once before immediately hoisting himself up and continuing.

At first, it seemed impossible, but as we approached what I believe to be the anchor point at Point Pleasant Park —where the old submarine net had once been chained to a boulder—the ice began to jam up a bit more and suddenly Garrett was making good headway.

Still paralyzed with the impossible nature of the situation, I watched as he gingerly crawled on all fours across the closest ice island and then dropped onto the frozen floor of the skiff. He was soaked and breathing harder than anyone I'd ever heard as he lay there for several long seconds, unable to speak.

His first words were, in retrospect, both heroic and absurd. "This is not a good day to die," he whispered as he tried to catch his breath. I think he borrowed it from some movie we had watched, although I never knew which one.

As we began to shift past the point of land with the anchor bolt, the ice began to break up. We were a little closer to shore now, but up ahead was much more open, choppy seawater.

Garrett heaved himself up off the floor of the boat. He grabbed me by the scruff of my neck and screamed, "Now!"

With that, he lifted me like a sack of potatoes and shoved me onto the closest ice pan. "Now get up, Nick. Move!" he screamed.

My legs did not want to work. The cold had seized up my muscles.

It was all happening so quickly, and I realized there was no time to do anything but my brother's bidding. I tried to walk but all I could do was stumble and slip on the now-shifting, now tilting ice pans.

We made some headway, but then the rising wind and a stronger current suddenly began to unpack the ice until there were no more ice islands to jump onto.

That's when Garrett made his leap of faith and threw himself into the water, screaming bloody murder. But he never let go his grip on my jacket collar.

We were blessedly close enough to shore that his feet found the bottom and he began dragging me through the horror of the freezing sea as chunks of ice slammed into us like someone hammering with angry fists.

My legs and hands were burning. My heart felt like it would burst. Garrett kept gasping for oxygen while I too huffed and puffed and wondered where my legs had gone.

And then we were ashore. I so wanted to lie down and try to figure out how to breathe again. But my brother was pounding on me.

"Gotta move. Gotta keep moving. We can't stay here," he gasped.

As I staggered to a somewhat standing position, I couldn't help but look back towards the little boat. If it was still afloat, I couldn't see it.

The ice pack was now moving swiftly out to sea and, with hypothermia no doubt setting into both of us, my brother instinctively knew he had to get us somewhere warm. If it had just been me, I might have just sat there staring at the icy sea and allowed myself to die of exposure, but fortunately Garrett had a different kind of stubbornness than mine. And he put it to work.

We hobbled along the shoreline until we came to one of those dead-end streets that run right down to the water. There was a car there with its engine idling. A black Subaru if I remember correctly.

A woman in a long fancy winter coat was getting out of the car and waving to us. Garrett waved back. She waved again for us to come to her.

I stared at her. She was smoking a cigarette and made no

effort to come our way to help, yet she kept waving for us to come to her between taking puffs on her smoke.

I suppose I was in a state of shock or hypothermia or whatever it is when a Canadian winter, the north wind, the Northwest Arm and the uncaring gods who look down on us all for amusement take great pleasure in our pain. Garrett had his fist locked onto my coat and he was dragging me towards her.

And just as Garrett was about to collapse, I watched as she tossed her cigarette and grabbed Garrett by his shoulder and heaved him into the backseat of her car.

She took a brief look at me and then slipped her arm under my armpit and hauled me around to the other side of the car, wrestled the door open, dropped me into the front passenger seat and slammed the door shut. Then she walked around and sat down behind the wheel.

With her car still idling, she cranked up the heat until it was blasting. The windows began to steam up immediately and I was thinking, *This is all so bizarre.*

I could do nothing at all but sit there and try to remember how to breathe.

5

"Take off your clothes," were the first words she spoke. "Both of you."

I was shaking uncontrollably at that point, and I may have been shaking all along. I just hadn't noticed. My hands were useless and, as she realized this, I watched as she unzipped my coat, unbuckled my belt, unsnapped the button of my Levis and worked the zipper down with deft hands.

"Kick your shoes off, dammit," she insisted.

Each frozen foot kicked at the other heel until my sneakers fell off and I struggled to get my pants off.

"How are you doing back there?" she asked my brother.

"Alive," Garrett answered, choking a bit. The word stuck in my head.

She started to unbutton my wet coat and tugged at it until the arms went inside out and she yanked me out of it. Then the shirt. I felt like a slab of frozen beef.

I listened as my brother struggled getting himself out of his clothes and the woman turned up the fan on the heater one more notch higher.

The pain of my toes and fingers thawing was excruciating, unlike anything I'd ever felt. It hurt so badly that I began to cry. I'm sorry, but that's what I did. How a person can still be embarrassed by crying after surviving an ordeal like that is a bit mystifying to me now, but there it is.

Stranger yet, I heard Garrett muffling his own tears in his backseat agony as he began to thaw as well.

"Jesus Christ," the woman said, cracking her window ever slightly to let some of the steam out. "What do you have to cry about? You're alive, aren't you?"

That word again.

I wanted to say something. But all I could think about was the pain of thawing out like this. Being alive apparently meant pain. A lot of it. It would not go away soon enough and, right then, it seemed so much worse than being stuck in the skiff floating all alone out to sea. I'm pretty sure both Garrett and I howled with the pain.

The woman cringed at the inhuman sounds we were making. Suddenly, she looked at me and then back at Garrett. It was an odd look. Annoyance maybe.

"You two are really making a mess of my car," she said as she reached for the pack of cigarettes on her dashboard, lit one and blew smoke through the side of her mouth out the open window.

As we continued to thaw, she turned on her CD player. It was the old Rolling Stones' "Sympathy for the Devil."

"You like the Stones?" she asked.

I don't think I had re-established any form of command of the language, so it was Garrett who sucked up what sounded like a large gobbet of snot and answered in a shaky voice, "I love the Rolling Stones."

The woman smiled, flicked some ash from her cigarette out the window and said, "They should never have tried to follow the Beatles into that psychedelic shit. 'Gimme Shelter' beats any of that crap by a country mile."

With that, she took her warm hand and slapped the inside of my frozen naked thigh. Had a woman touched me there at any other time of my young life, I might have thought it a gold star day, but there and then it just seemed downright strange.

So my brother and I sat there, still thawing as the pain subsided, and listened to Mick sing:

> Ah, what's puzzling you
> Is the nature of my game, oh yeah.

At the end of the song, the woman punched a button that stopped the music and held out her hand. "I'm Marlene," she said. "Any port in a storm."

My brother was still shaking as he cleared his throat and introduced us. "I'm Garrett and this is my idiot little brother, Nicky."

"Pleased to meet yas," she said. "Now tell me, how the fuck did you end up in the water?"

Garrett tried to explain as best he could, but she just kept shaking her head, dragging on her cigarette and laughing, after which she asked, "Shall I take you two sailors home to your mommy or you wanna just drive around Halifax in your underwear for a while?"

"I think I'd like to go home now," I piped up.

Marlene took a final drag on her cigarette and flicked it out the open window onto the driveway.

At home, Marlene carried our wet clothes and walked us

to the front door. When we spilled into the front hallway, my mother looked at us in shock.

Marlene dropped our wet clothes on the floor and said to my mom, "I'd keep these two out of the pool for a while." And she started to walk away.

"No," Garrett said. "Stay. Come in."

Marlene looked a little confused.

It was the first time I got a good look at her. She was quite attractive in a tough sort of way and wore a lot of make-up. That coat she had on—was it fake fur or real? It wasn't like anything my mom or my mom's friends would ever wear.

Garrett tried to explain what had happened and why her two sons were showing up at home so bedraggled, shivering in their underwear. But my mom just kind of stood there in disbelief until she gathered us in her arms and gave us a big hug. I thought my bones were going to shatter.

When the confusion began to settle a bit and my mother understood that her sons had survived a life-threatening ordeal but were now safely home, she invited the bemused Marlene in for a cup of Earl Grey.

By the time Garrett and I had showered, put on dry clothes and tiptoed downstairs, Marlene and our mother were sipping tea, eating slices of homemade brown bread and laughing. The first words I heard my mother asking her were, "What exactly does an exotic dancer do?"

As Marlene explained in most modest terms her occupation as "someone who performs a specialized kind of dance at private parties," she added, "You know, your boys are about the politest young men I've ever encountered."

6

By now you must be thinking, hey wait, this isn't Nick's story at all. This is about his hero brother, the golden boy, Garrett.

Well, it is and it isn't.

And don't start thinking Garrett is like the Great Gatsby of my family. Yes, I read the damn book, Mr. Tasker. I've read a lot more books than you can imagine and I'm willing to let you in on that secret, but please don't tell those other shitheads who teach at our school. I mean, I had to have something to do while I was ignoring my homework, cutting classes and skipping school. There are libraries out there, aren't there? And they have scads of books. Some even worth reading.

If someone other than Mr. T is reading this, then *this* might even be one of them.

And there's more about Garrett, much more.

But first, let me take you back to that scene of my mom sitting in our kitchen with this lady who had just stripped my brother and me of our wet clothes in her car.

"Being an exotic dancer is just a job like any other," Marlene casually explained, rolling a fresh cigarette around in her hand but being polite enough not to light it.

"Really?" my mom asked, wide-eyed.

"Yes."

Mom said nothing. I heard Garrett swallow loudly.

Marlene said, "The pay is good. The hours suck. The men in the audience suck. But it's what I do to make ends meet."

At which point she rolled the cigarette between her fingers a little too energetically and it flipped onto the table.

Mom took a desperate sip of her tea, took a deep breath, and said, "God bless you for helping my boys."

"No problem. Just tell your sons to keep off the ice from now on. Don't you have video games or something safe to keep them out of trouble?"

This made my mom laugh, because she hated video games the same way some people hate Hitler or heart disease. But the laughing only lasted a few seconds and then she began to cry. She didn't have to say what she was thinking: *They could have died out there.*

So while these two unlikely-paired women are sipping the dregs of their tea, let's consider how this could have played out otherwise.

Well, one scenario has me all alone in that stupid little boat, locked into the ice and drifting right out to sea. Straight out the harbour, past Devil's Island. But I don't think the boat would have made it too far. It would have sunk.

Maybe I would have made it up onto a really big ice pan and hunkered down. But I would have been wet and cold and died of exposure. And that would be that. Who would miss me really, other than Mom and Garrett? Garrett would have been scarred for life, probably, blaming himself.

Or maybe Garrett would have joined me as we drifted out, too far from shore to make it safely back. I'm pretty sure he would have figured out something, but I don't know what.

At that stage in his life, he always seemed to come out of anything bad unscathed. Skateboard accidents. Bully threats. Any number of boyhood adventures that turned ugly. He just always found a way to "turn shit into sunshine," as he liked to say.

So we could have drifted all the way to Sable Island if we didn't freeze to death. And there we'd have settled down among the ponies in the dunes or built a little cabin out of driftwood, assuming there is driftwood on Sable Island. It could have been an adventure.

But I guess me telling my story and Garrett's story isn't really about all the what-ifs, is it? Because if it was, we could be at this into the next century—assuming there is a next century. Of which I'm not so sure.

Okay, back on track.

After that icy near-disaster something changed. Garrett began to change. And I blame her.

Yes, Marlene. The exotic dancer.

Let me remind you, I was twelve, Garrett was fifteen going on sixteen. And that night, after our fingers were no longer numb, after our frozen legs had stopped itching from thawing out, after our mom had pulled her shit together and stopped talking about "what could have happened to my boys," after she broke her vegetarian code of ethics and bought us a meat-lover's pizza from Pizza Hut, well, that's when Garrett said something that freaked me out.

"I think I'm in love."

Now that I'm older and wiser and can look back on this with some degree of intellectual understanding, I can say in no uncertain terms, when you are fifteen going on sixteen and you *think* you are in love, there's not much difference between thinking and being.

I thought he was joking, of course. Garrett liked to joke, once upon a time. He liked to say outrageous things just to get a response. He liked to say that one day he'd be President of the United States, even though he was Canadian. "I can be whatever I want to be if I set my mind to it," he said.

He meant it, of course, and I know that sounds like the bold words of some poster boy for something or other. But if things had turned out differently, he might have figured out a way to become President of the United States by twenty-one. (I think you have to be like thirty-five years old before you can become president, but I'm not sure.) And it was just like him not to want to be Canada's Prime Minister but an American president. He always set his goals a bit higher than anyone else.

"You can't be serious," I said.

"I am serious. I'm going to marry her."

I expected him to whack me on the shoulder then and say he was joking.

"You're joking, right?"

"No. I'm serious."

"Shut up and go to sleep. Stop talking nonsense."

Garrett suddenly got mad at me. This was not like him at all. And I think that somehow him getting mad at me was a pivotal moment in his transformation. Or maybe it happened earlier when we were sitting cold and wet in Marlene's car while she flicked cigarette ash out the window. Whatever moment it was, it happened that day.

That damn day.

I didn't know what to say to my infatuated brother. I was only twelve. I had *liked* girls and one or two of them had said they *liked* me, even though I was pretty hard to like. I was about as hard-headed as they come back then. (Well, I still am.) I mean, I refused to tie my shoelaces right up to twelve years old. Why? Just because. My poor mom gave up telling me to lace up and just started buying me running shoes with those Velcro straps.

Now that I'm this far into the story, I think that maybe Garrett should be telling it. "How I Fell in Love with an Older Woman", or some shit like that.

But no, now that I see that dumb idea in writing, I guess it's up to me.

7

After that day, I went back to being me. You'd think a nearly-fatal event like drifting out to sea in a sinking skiff among slob ice would make me see the world in a whole new light. But it didn't. I pretty much had one gear forward, and that was obstinate. Hard-headed, hopeless Nicholas.

But it was worse than usual. I'd lost my guiding star. Garrett.

Mom was working long hours at the organic food store now. We were eating the day-old stuff or the almost-over-the-hill veggies. I had given up on refusing to eat the food she brought home because it was obvious, even to me back then, that if I didn't eat something, I'd get even skinnier than I already was and maybe starve to death. There was a very thin line between kale quiche and death by starvation, so I had to give in to the kale.

I found a video game in somebody's trash and took it home, hooked it up when no one else was around and shot video bullets at enemy soldiers for hours. Then I hid the game before Mom got home.

And Garrett? Well, that's the thing. He started hanging out at Marlene's house. Fifteen turned into sixteen, as it often does, and Garrett stood taller, less stooped over, and acted less like a kid and more like whatever it is that adults act like. He paid more attention to the way he looked. His clothes, his hair, that pathetic display of lip hair he liked to call his moustache.

Several afternoons a week, Garrett was gone visiting Marlene. I know what you're thinking, but back then I'm sure it was just some kind of weird friendship. My mom was worried about it, and she'd call up Marlene sometimes and have a heart-to-heart talk with her, and whatever Marlene said, it made Mom feel better and for a while she would stop trying to prevent Garrett from hanging out with the professional exotic dancer.

A teenage boy in love with an older woman: most anyone can tell you, is not a good thing. I reckoned Marlene to be in her late twenties. And she was quite beautiful but not in that magazine sort of way. Not quite the girl (or lady) next door, but certainly not your Aunt Edna or anything like that.

And before you go jumping to any conclusions, I don't think Marlene was really doing anything wrong. It's all very strange, I know. Garrett was in love with the woman, yes. He probably wanted more than she was offering, but he wasn't getting it. Marlene just liked having the company of someone who thought she was the greatest thing on earth.

But Garrett's grades started dropping. And he was spending way too much time at her house. I felt like I had truly lost my brother. My anchor had drifted away. Thanks to shoot 'em up video games, stubbornness and a lack of interest in most anything, I was on the road to being just another stupid, lazy teenager. Well, I *was* a stupid lazy teenager and was quite pleased with being just that.

The school counsellor had explained to both me and my mom that I had some kind of learning disorder. He had a fancy term for it—a kind of hybrid deficiency involving various quadrants of my brain. Something to do with a lobe and a cortex and the way that my eyes were not correctly reporting to my brain the information that they should be. He told my mom this could be fixed with drugs or therapy.

She opted for therapy, but it turned out that the therapist really pissed me off with something he said. And I threw several large medical texts through the glass front of a bookcase. It cost my mom a bundle to replace, and that was the end of that.

By then I was thirteen, which is not a happy age to be, I discovered. There were many things wrong with the world as I saw it, and I didn't want to be part of it. I really didn't.

I'm not talking about suicide here. I just wanted my own world, my own way. Most thirteen-year-olds probably feel the same way. Even now, I still wish I could create my own world. But now, as then, I was stuck with the damn one that I was born into.

Not long after the book-throwing, glass-breaking psychiatric incident, Garrett suddenly seemed to remember that he had a little brother. He was looking at himself in the mirror in our bedroom at the time, counting the hairs on his lip, I think, or brushing his unruly mop of hair. And he suddenly stopped and asked, "How are things going with you, Nick?"

"Hopeless as usual," I answered.

He looked concerned, like he suddenly remembered that I was what they called a troubled youth, an incorrigible student, a blighted boy.

"You should come to Marlene's with me tomorrow. Maybe she can help."

Tomorrow was Saturday, and most Saturdays Garrett disappeared to Marlene's until nearly dark.

"Okay," I said. "But what do you do over there all the time?" I was almost afraid of how he was going to answer.

"Talk. We mostly talk."

"That's a lot of talking."

"There's a lot to talk about."

"Are you still in love with her?"

Garrett didn't like my question. He looked away. He ran his hand through his hair. "Yes, I am."

"Holy Christ," I said. "Is she in love with you?"

Now he spun around so he was looking in the opposite direction of me. More fiddling with his hair. "I don't know," he finally said. Then he added, "It doesn't matter."

I tried to make sense of that. But I couldn't.

~

Marlene was reading a book when we arrived. *Zen and the Art of Motorcycle Maintenance* was the title. She didn't seem at all surprised to see me.

The house smelled of weed. It was the kind of sweet, skunky smell I'd come across down at the skateboard park. I think it was maybe one of those left-over smells like from the night before.

I didn't really think much of it. Cannabis was legal and my mom even took small amounts of CBH oil, which she had explained did not make her high but helped with her occasional anxiety.

Anyway, there we were in Marlene's house, and she set her book down and smiled at me. "You know, Nick, the first time I met you, you looked like a skinny drowned rat."

She had a great smile. And not a lot of people smile at me, so, despite the drowned rat part, I suddenly felt right at home there.

"I thought he should come along," Garrett said.

"The more the merrier," Marlene chimed. "You two want something to drink?"

"I'll take a beer," Garrett said. And I thought, *Oh shit. Now my brother's drinking.*

Marlene opened her fridge and tossed a can of Bud Lite to Garrett. "What about you, Nicholas?" She used my formal name.

"Me too," I said.

"Don't be foolish," she said, tossing me a can of Diet Coke. "Sit, everybody."

Garrett cracked open his Bud and we all sat down on the creaky wooden chairs around the kitchen table.

Marlene was drinking a glass of water with ice cubes in it and kept swirling the ice cubes around with her index finger. An unopened pack of smokes was on the table.

She noticed I was staring at it. "I'm trying to stop," she said. "Isn't that what all smokers say? I'm trying. And then we get weak and say, fuck it, and then we smoke."

"You really should stop smoking," Garrett said.

Marlene gave him a look. "Don't come here and tell me what to do."

"Sorry."

"Forget it. I know you're just trying to look out for me."

Then she turned to me. "Your brother's like that, right? He likes looking out for people. You're lucky to have him."

"I know," I said, even though Garrett had stopped "looking out for me" ever since Marlene came into the picture.

I watched my brother slug back the beer. There was a moment of awkward silence while Marlene started to fiddle with the unopened pack of cigarettes and Garrett took another gulp of beer. And I was thinking, *This is freaking weird. Here it is Saturday morning and I'm sitting in the kitchen of an "exotic dancer", watching my sixteen-year-old brother drinking beer.*

"Garrett tells me he once wanted to be President of the United States."

Garrett looked a little embarrassed. "And then an astronaut," he added. "First man on Mars, to be precise."

"Awe...that would be sad," she said, putting her hand on his. "If you were on Mars, you wouldn't be able to come visit me." She said it in a very sexy way.

"Maybe you can come with me," Garrett said.

"Maybe," she cooed. "What about you, Nicholas? Astronaut, world leader, rock star or techno-genius of some sort?"

"I really haven't given it much thought," I said. Then I took a big mouthful of Coke which tickled my nose.

Marlene tapped the cover of the book on the table. "I think you're the intellectual type. You should be a writer."

The Coke nearly shot out of my nose. No one, I mean no one, had ever called me the intellectual type before. And a writer? Who was she kidding? I was getting straight Ds in

English.

When I recovered, I asked her, "What would I write about?"

"Me," she said. "You could write the story of my life. Or I could be your muse and inspire you to write."

I was sure, however, she had said 'moose' and not 'muse', and that was pretty funny. The Coke really did spray out of my left nostril that time.

"Muse, idiot," Garrett said, slapping me on the back. "Someone who inspires."

"Oh."

Marlene laughed now. "He thought I said moose. I get it. I like that better. Sure, I'll be your moose and you can write about me. Let me go find my antlers."

I can't recall all the conversation after that, but I guess the right word is banter. Silly, unimportant conversation about everything and anything.

The beer loosened Garrett's tongue. He kept asking Marlene questions and giving her compliments, and she was absorbing every bit of it. It was quite a show. The time just slipped by.

Marlene and Garrett seemed happy in each other's company. He had a second beer. She just sipped at her ice water.

And then the conversation just sort of petered out. Marlene picked up the cigarette pack, used her long nails to cut the cellophane, tapped out a single cigarette and lit it with a lighter that was perched on the edge of the sink.

"Work really is getting to me," she said, after taking a long drag. "I'm thinking I need some kind of different work. A different life, maybe. I'm getting too old for this."

8

Marlene did not quit her job. Not then, anyway.

Other things were changing, though. I don't mean me. I was pretty much a constant. I was a pain in the academic ass at school, as usual. No one, including myself, could really understand why I refused to participate in school activities or do homework or do anything "productive" during a school day other than try to bust the chops of my teachers.

By now I was thirteen going on fourteen, and had grown quite a bit during that year.

Growth spurts, they call them. So, inside I was still pretty much the little twerp I always had been. Smart-alecky, wise-cracking, rarely saying anything to anybody other than a sarcastic remark, a snarky quip or an unkind word. I was the king of the unkind word. I honed my skills and used them against my fellow school inmates and the so-called teachers who were well paid to be our jailers.

But because of my growth spurt—brought on, according to my mother, by eating healthy organic food—I could now intimidate others if I wanted. Even my teachers.

Intimidation wasn't really my shtick, but it was good for fending off the familiar louts who had so often been on my case during my wonder years. In fact, now that I had girth and grit, I could bully them on occasion to even up a score.

But soon I found this to require too much effort and, on top of my many other disagreeable traits, I was lazy.

Each Saturday I was permitted to go along with Garrett to visit Marlene, and one day she asked me why I was doing so poorly in school.

"Just lazy, I guess," I said, not wanting to put too much effort into thinking about an honest answer.

Marlene was moving a little slow that Saturday morning. Sometimes she could have been a bit hungover from a staff party with her dancing "sisters," as she called them, at two in the morning. Other times, I smelled the scent of marijuana on her. But she never brought out the weed when I was there. On this morning, she didn't like my wimpy answer about being lazy.

"Never say that," she countered, suddenly fiery-eyed, beautiful, animated, opinionated and sexy all at once.

"Why?" I asked in my traditional smart-ass way.

"Because, youthful idiot, you become the person you perceive yourself to be."

Aside from the youthful idiot part, it sounded like something out of the old university psychology textbooks that Marlene loaned to Garrett.

Yes, Marlene was devout reader of any book she could lay her hands for less than 50 cents at a yard sale or a Value Village store. Including textbooks. She loaned or gave them to Garrett, he would read every word and, when he was finished with them, he loaned them to me. "But you have to give them back," he'd often say. "Marlene gave them to me."

So, strangely enough, stranger than fiction could ever be,

Garrett and I became great readers of university textbooks on psychology, biology, sociology, philosophy and anthropology. At first, I was just looking at the pictures and captions, but then I started to get more interested.

Marlene was also a big fan of the classics and if you think I'm lying when I say I read *Crime and Punishment* by Dostoevsky when I had just turned fourteen, just test me.

None of this reading, to my way of thinking, related to school, where I was now cruising along at a C or C- average, probably doing that well by a kind of mental osmosis by just being around Marlene and reading her second-hand books. (Third-hand, really, after being passed down by my older brother.)

At school, I got shifted into what they called a "special" class. That term special kept cropping up in education, meaning a number of different things according to what the current trend was. I, of course, had read a couple of university education textbooks and found most of the ideas interesting but bone-headed. So I had some kind of idea as to what this was all about.

We "special" ones were sort of the bottom of the heap academically, each of us for our own reason. Me, my reason was inherited stubbornness and what I liked to think of as an independent spirit. (No brainwashing for Nicholas. Not on your life.)

Oh, and Marlene had given me a new word. "Never say lazy, Nicky. And stop calling yourself hopeless. Incorrigible, maybe. But that can be said of many of the great minds of the human race."

So maybe I *was* in my special special class because I was

incorrigible. And just for the record, that meant I was bad and could not be changed.

Marlene, however, often said things like, "Everything changes. That's the only constant." I think she was quoting someone, but she claimed she had made it up.

I'd sometimes counter that and say, "Yeah, everything but me," and she'd give me a look.

Well, enough about school. Suffice it to say the system never knew what to do with me and was way too polite to simply kick me out on my ass, give me the royal academic middle finger and tell me to go live my life on the street.

Aside from Marlene, Garrett and I had no social life. But then, from what I could see, aside from Garrett and me, Marlene had no social life. "I'm off men," she said once when Garrett asked her if she thought she'd ever marry.

Garrett and I looked at each other. It had never occurred to us.

Marlene saw the look. "No," she said. "I see that. I'm not gay. At least, I don't think I am. Although I've considered it. What if I was? What would you think then?"

I knew better than to answer.

Garrett jumped in. "That would be okay. We wouldn't care."

Marlene laughed. She had a great laugh, but it sometimes ended in a smoker's cough, which we both worried about.

"No. The big problem is my job doesn't exactly allow me to see the best side of the male of the species."

I could understand that. We had both figured out a long time ago that an exotic dancer was pretty much the same as a stripper, but we didn't want to discuss such a thing.

"And, besides, I've been married twice. Didn't work out well either time."

"Third time's the charm," I piped up, mouthing something I'd heard in a movie.

More laughing, more coughing.

~

Of course, I was only allowed into the sacred circle on Saturdays, and I suppose it was only the loyalty of my older brud that permitted that to happen. And I had to admit after a while that I was probably almost in love with Marlene as much as my brother was. But I'll stick to "almost."

And if you are still thinking that Marlene and Garrett had some kind of illicit older woman/ younger guy sexual thing going, I will state, unequivocally, I believe that to be untrue.

But I can't prove it.

My mom asked a lot of questions about this business with Marlene, but Garrett always had good answers. What I am almost dead sure were true answers.

But Marlene was not just our friend. It was much more than that. And the fact that I'm writing this is not just because of the carrot-on-a-stick graduation thing from Tasker. I guess you could say Marlene *is* my muse. She's still in my head. Make of that what you may.

To quote Dostoevsky, "Love in action is a harsh and dreadful thing compared with love in dreams." If you get my drift.

But then, he also said, "The greatest happiness is to know the source of unhappiness." And I wouldn't have known any of this had Marlene not been my inspiration and my true teacher.

"You need to identify the source of your unhappiness," she told me. "Then work with it."

What the hell was the source of my unhappiness, anyway? I thought long and hard about this and dug into those old philosophy texts to see what great minds had said about unhappiness.

"There are no happy surfaces without terrible depth," said Nietzsche in one of his contemplative moments. But that certainly didn't apply to me.

I didn't see myself as a very deep person.

9

If I had been using my wits more, I would have paid less at-tention to how so many things in the world annoyed me and more attention to what was happening to my brother. That ice incident had changed him in some profound way that I could never quite understand.

Maybe he had fully realized that we were both mortal. No, that sounds silly. True, we could have died that day. Drifted to sea and drowned.

That would have ended this story before it even began. How many dead teenagers get to tell their own story?

But it wasn't just the drift ice, the skiff, the north wind, the bloody cold. The world conspires a thousand conspir-acies to kill us off. It's not really a plot. It's the indifferent forces of nature. Or it's the greed and hatred of humans. Or it's some other damn thing. The result is the same.

The only reason we survived was the luck of drifting past that little bit of Nova Scotia land that stuck out into the wa-ter before we reached the open ocean. That and Garrett's willingness to act. And to drag me along to save my ass.

I couldn't have done it. My show would have ended. Mom would have grieved, and some folks would have said how tragic and sad it all was, and then the world would have moved on.

But the ice didn't really change Garrett. Marlene did.

And I can't say it was her fault. And it would be glib of me to say that because of Marlene he somehow changed from being a boy into being a man. None of that shit.

But some powerful force threw a switch in his brain. He became less outward and more inward, if I can say it that way. He stopped seeing the world as a big playground and started taking it seriously. He started taking himself seriously.

I missed the old Garrett. But there was nothing I could do to reverse the process.

One evening over dinner, my mom said we were getting tight on money. She had a small raise at the health food store, but it wasn't much. Our rent kept going up. Our old Chevy had bit the dust.

Clearly, Mom was pretty stressed-out about money, so Garrett took a job hauling in shopping carts from the parking lot at the Superstore on Barrington Street after school. He claimed he liked the job, but it meant he had less time for Marlene.

My mom confided in me that she thought that was all for the good. She pretended, though, that she wasn't worried about Garrett's friendship with Marlene, and she always claimed that she trusted him, but sometimes confided in me that she felt it was "a little odd."

In Garrett's defence, I tried to convince her that it was all perfectly okay. But I, too, thought it was a bit unusual.

And truth was, I was jealous that Garrett got to spend more time with her than me. This most unusual and interesting woman had come into our lives in a most unusual way, and she had become some kind of weird and wonderful anchor for both my brother and myself.

Due to his job, Garrett missed visiting Marlene two Saturdays in a row. The first time, I stayed home, too.

But when he had to work a second Saturday, he said to me, "Nick, you better go see her on your own. You know how she hates to be alone on Saturday."

"I don't think so," I said. I'd never been alone with Marlene. I was always my brother's sidekick. My wingman, he called me, although I never quite understood the reference. "I wouldn't know what to say."

"You always have something to say, idiot. You two talk about those books. You listen to her stories, and you always agree with her about how fucked up the world is. You'll be fine."

"No, it wouldn't feel right."

He just shook his head. "Suit yourself."

When Saturday morning rolled around, my mom was working a weekend shift at Organic Planet, and I was home alone. TV, internet and video games just weren't doing it for me anymore.

So I walked over there, all the while wondering what we would talk about. I was nervous. I'd never had Marlene all to myself. It was Garrett who was her friend, her confidant. I was just the little brother.

I rang the bell.

Nothing.

I knocked on the door.

Nothing.

She'd always told us to just walk in. And we always did. Sometimes she was still asleep, and we'd sit in the kitchen and wait for her to wake up. She was always happy to see us when she shuffled into the kitchen. Always.

Sometimes, Garrett would make the coffee and it'd be sitting waiting for her when she came in. She'd smile that amazing smile and then give my brother a hug. I watched when that happened, and his eyes went funny.

The door was unlocked. Always was.

So I walked in.

Nobody. Nothing. The faint musky odour of weed, probably from the night before. Marlene always said that she had a hard time sleeping. A couple of puffs of something she called candy kush would do it, though, put her right out into dreamland.

I felt nervous and scared, but I couldn't really understand why.

There was the coffee maker. I opened a cabinet and found the coffee and the box of filters. I'd watched Garrett do this. I could handle it. My first pot of coffee.

But what if she woke up, came in and found only me, not Garrett? Would she be upset? Would she say, *What the hell are you doing here?* What if I was stepping over some kind of boundary?

There was a paperback book open on the scarred wooden table, face down with a cracked spine. Marlene was always hard on books. It was *The Bell Jar* by Sylvia Plath. I'd never heard of it.

I picked it up and flipped back to the first page, read the first line. "It was a queer, sultry summer, the summer they electrocuted the Rosenbergs, and I didn't know what I was doing in New York."

That didn't mean much of anything to me. Who were the Rosenbergs? *Queer*—well, didn't that mean, what? Gay, right? Sultry? I'd come across that before in another novel she had loaned me. Hot and humid, I think. But something else too. "Of a passionate nature" was the polite way the online dictionary put it.

Did the men at Marlene's "club" consider her sultry? Did it also mean sexy?

I was wondering if Marlene would pass this one along to me when she was finished with it, cracked spine and all. So many of her hand-me-down books had the same damage.

The coffeemaker steamed and hissed as it dripped. I wondered if I had put in the proper amount of coffee grounds. Five scoops? I was hoping Marlene wouldn't be disappointed.

And then it occurred to me she might not even be home. She never locked her door. Something about "not having anything worth stealing." And Garrett and I had not shown up last Saturday, so maybe she was somewhere else. And if so, what the hell was I doing in her house, sitting at her kitchen table, making coffee and reading the first line of her novel?

Shit. Maybe I should just leave. But not before turning off the coffee maker. What exactly should I do?

What seemed like the thing to do was to check and see if she was in the house. Check to see if she was just sleeping. Make sure at least that, if she was here, she was okay. The proper thing to do, right? I didn't know, and without Garrett here to make all the usual Garrett decisions, I was on my own.

So I quietly walked out of the kitchen and down the little hallway with all the books piled up along the walls. The floorboards creaked. The smell of cannabis was a bit stronger. The door to her bedroom was open just a crack as I leaned forward to peer in.

There she was. Marlene. Covers bunched up around her, her head on a pillow with a dingy pillowcase, snoring. Loudly.

I stood there, frozen. Somehow this all seemed rather surreal. Here I was alone in Marlene's unlocked house standing at her bedroom door watching her sleep. In truth, it was a bit exciting. But then it immediately occurred to me that this was also a bit… what? Weird? For certain. Creepy? You bet. Shit, maybe it was time to leave without a trace.

But I'd already made the coffee and I'd likely wake her if I tried to pour it down the sink and clean up. Damn. What a crazy situation. But did I really want to leave?

I was thinking, H*ere's this crazy beautiful woman sound asleep in her bed in an unlocked house. Shouldn't I at least stay and watch over her? Like a good protector, like a good gentleman?*

I think I stopped breathing. But as I leaned a little closer my head bumped into the door, and it swung open. Oh shit. More creaking.

That's when she woke up.

She seemed to have a hard time getting her eyes focused, but when she did, she bolted upright in bed and stared straight at me.

"Nicholas."

"I'm sorry," I said, taking a step back out of the room and accidentally kicking over one of those piles of books in the hallway.

"Get back in here," she said.

I dutifully walked back in.

"What are you doing here?"

"It's Saturday," I said.

"I know that. But I figured you two had given up on me and had discovered better things to do. You didn't show up last Saturday."

You'd think that maybe in all the time we'd known each other there would have been phone calls or text messages. But that had never happened. Neither Garrett or me had a cell phone. My mom had the only family cell phone and there was no land line at home. We had a computer but were probably the only family in our neighbourhood with no internet. I had stopped asking about it. If I wanted to Google anything, I'd go to the public library like a homeless person. So Marlene and her two doting teenagers only communicated face to face.

"Where's Garrett?"

"Working."

"So you came alone?" She sounded suspicious.

I nodded.

"And let yourself in?"

I nodded again.

"Did you make me coffee?"

"I did," I answered.

And then she smiled. It was a smile that lit up the room.

A word for it jumped into my head. The word was *incandescent.*

"Thank God," she said. "Now get out of here so I can get dressed and I'll join you in the kitchen."

10

"I thought I'd been abandoned," she said, walking into the kitchen in a heavy quilted robe not unlike what my mother would wear around the house. A housecoat, I guess you could call it.

"We're kind of tight for money," I said. "Garrett really needs to work."

"Doesn't your father kick in some money for you guys?"

"Never did. Once he left, he was just gone. As in *gone* gone."

"Another deadbeat dad. I've met more than my share. They come into the club and drop a hundred dollars on drinks, then ask me to sit with them so they can complain about their lives or their ex-wives and the divorce."

"I don't know if he's like that. Maybe. I really can hardly remember him."

Marlene was pouring coffee now. On the side of the cup were the words "Nova Scotia Strong." It was the cup she always used.

She poured more coffee into a cup that had the inscription "2020 WTF?" She set it in front of me even though I'd told her a dozen times I don't drink coffee. It makes me hyper, and no one wants to be around me when I'm hyper.

"Why'd he leave? Your father."

"I think he left because of me." I wasn't about to explain about the toilet training or any of the other difficulties I presented as a rat rug for two parents already struggling in a relationship.

"I doubt it. Men leave for all kinds of selfish reasons. The whole lot of them are shits."

Like I said, Marlene was "off men."

But as I sat, with my hands cupped around the 2020 WTF? mug, feeling the warmth, I rather empathized with her but also wondered how Garrett and I fit into the picture. Were we still too young to be corrupted by impending manhood?

Marlene was looking around the kitchen now. "You didn't see my smokes, did you?"

They had been strategically placed on top of the coffee maker. I had had to move them to make the coffee. "No," I said.

"Liar."

She spotted them by the sink, got up to retrieve them, then did one of her familiar routines of setting the unopened pack of Players on the table in front of her and helicoptering around it with her long, slender fingers.

"So Garrett's working and you're here to keep Marlene company?"

"Something like that."

"You read some of those recent books I gave you?"

"I did."

"Don't worry. You don't have to give me a book report or anything."

"Some of the novels were kind of depressing."

"Life is depressing."

"I keep thinking there should be something more." I'm not sure where that came from, but that's what I came away with from reading the books Marlene loaned me. They were all so serious. "How come you read so many depressing stories?"

"They, my good friend, are considered classics. I studied literature in university."

"You did?"

"Don't look so surprised. A lot of young women put themselves through university by stripping."

It was the very first time she had ever used the word. I wouldn't question it.

"It doesn't seem right," I said, not sure of what I meant. "It doesn't seem fair."

She laughed. My God, that woman could let loose when she laughed. Until the laugh turned into a cough and she had to stop herself. "Didn't your mother tell you life wasn't fair?"

"No."

"Hey, don't get me wrong. I haven't had it the best, but I've had it better than a lot of my co-workers. I don't have a shit boyfriend who beats me up. I can pay my own way. I've had it okay. Only trouble is, all that's about to change."

"What do you mean?"

She noticed I hadn't taken a sip of the coffee. "You really don't drink coffee?"

"No. What did you mean about things changing?"

She looked away from me as if staring out at something

through the window over the sink, but there was nothing out there but grey sky. "I quit last night. It was, as they say, my time."

"You quit?"

"I have some things I have to deal with."

"What kind of things?" Who was I to be asking?

"Health things."

"Oh shit," I said out loud.

"Nothing to worry about."

"What is it?"

"Forget it. I don't want to talk about it."

I took a sip of the coffee. It was strong and bitter. Tasted like shit.

"Trouble is, I have to go away. Some kind of treatment I can't get here."

"Treatment," I repeated.

"You don't need to know."

I was wondering why she was telling me any of this. It should have been Garrett she was opening up to, not me. But here I was. And now she was confiding in me that she had something wrong. And that she had to go away.

"Yeah, I do need to know," I insisted. That was the old me, the usual me, kicking in. Asking the question that someone didn't want me to ask. Being insistent. Obstinate. Pain in the ass.

"Glioblastoma multiforme. GBM for short."

"I don't understand. It sounds bad."

"It is bad. But it could be the doctors here are wrong. It could be benign. Either way I need to go home to Vancouver to a specialist who can do something about it. They just don't have the right equipment here."

"Are you talking about cancer?"

"If it's GBM, yes, but if I'm lucky it will be this other thing —craniopharyngiomas. That's what I'm hoping for. Ever hear a person say, 'Geez, I sure hope I have craniopharyngiomas?'"

"Because that would be good, right? Benign?"

"Yes, that would be good."

"But if it's not?"

She picked up the cigarettes now and that freaked me out. So I reached over and grabbed them from her, spilling some of my coffee as I did so.

This angered Marlene. "Hey. Cool it."

"You shouldn't."

"Well, I shouldn't do a lot of things. But I doubt it was the smokes that did this to me. They think it is genetic. A gift from my ancestors."

I wiped at the coffee spill with my hand.

"I'm sorry, I shouldn't have told you. But whatever is going on in my head—and that's where the problem is, in case it didn't connect—whatever it is, I have to go away for a while and you and Garrett at least needed to know why.

"I've been down this road before. I had breast cancer a few years back. Had chemo and everything. Kind of ironic, don't you think?" She had both of her hands on her chest now. "My boobs were what got me the job dancing. And they were what gave me my first big health scare."

She had never used that term before. Another first. And not a good one.

"I got past that. Chemo did the trick. Even kept dancing.

The boss noticed I was a little pale, and I had to wear a wig because my hair mostly fell out. Wouldn't that have been a lark, dancing as a bald-headed woman? Shit, I just wore the wig. A cheap one. Long platinum hair. The guys loved it. I always wanted to whip it off right in the middle of a show."

I guess I looked stunned because she said, "Hey, Nick, you still there?"

"I'm still here."

"Take that look off your face. This is just some shit I have to do. Like, you know, going to the dentist and stuff like that."

"I don't think it's the same thing. What do I tell Garrett?"

Marlene got up to pour herself some more coffee and stare out the window up at the sky. "Tell him what I told you. Listen, you guys are two of the most polite, kindest teenagers I ever met in my life. I have always liked hanging out with you."

"But we could never figure out why."

"That's easy. You never wanted anything from me. Garrett always has that puppy dog look, I know. And so do you. But you are just a couple of people who I feel comfortable to be around. In case you didn't notice, I don't really have any friends."

"What about family?"

"I grew up in Vancouver, where I had been adopted. Well, actually it was a series of foster parents who mostly did it for the money. Can't say I bonded with any of them or them with me. Loner girl from the get-go. I could handle that. I came down here to get away from the rat race, but ended up doing the only thing I seemed to be good at. Got through university reading all those books, but it didn't seem to help in the employment department. So, here I am, a thirty-two-year-old woman, about to leave behind a career of wiggling my ass in public, and now what?"

I was still trying to get my head around all the news she was delivering. Soon she'd be gone. Soon she'd be in medical treatment on the other side of the country. Garrett was going to lose it. I was already feeling the loss. Already feeling a chill of dread as to what might happen to Marlene.

But Garrett. Garrett was *not* going to be able to handle this.

I leaned back in my chair and pushed the coffee cup slightly away. "But I still don't get it. Why us? Why did you open your door to Garrett any time he wanted to come over here, and you even let me tag along?"

"Garrett is like no one I ever met, if you want to know the truth. You know there's something special about him, right? I knew it from the first time we talked together. But the timing was all off. Jesus, we're sixteen years apart and I knew that nothing was going to come from it. But he was a blessed reminder that there are good people out there. Good *guys*. And you, Nick, you are like an even younger version of him. The two of you make me very happy when you are here. I never feel pressured. I always feel accepted for who I am. I don't think anyone else ever made me feel that way."

I didn't know what to say. I was nothing like Garrett. In fact, we were just about as opposite as two brothers could be. But what she said shook up my world. Turned it upside down.

I sat in silence and watched as Marlene tossed her un-opened pack of cigarettes into the sink.

"Besides," she continued. "You two daring dopes would have frozen to death if I hadn't set you down in my Honda and stripped the wet clothes off you. Because I saved your sorry asses, I felt a certain responsibility for you. So my door was always open."

11

"I gotta take a shower," Marlene said, standing up and tilting back her head.

"I guess I should go."

"No, stay. I'll cook you something to eat."

She looked at the clock. Eleven a.m. "Brunch, right? You'll stay and join me for brunch. I still have some things I need to talk about with you."

"No, I think I should go." Marlene had opened up to me—just me—in a way she had never done before, and I was feeling overwhelmed.

"Stay," she insisted, and left the room.

So I stayed.

It was a very short shower. She had left the door open, but I didn't look.

She deeked back into her bedroom and put on some jeans and an old flannel shirt. When she came into the kitchen, she had a towel around her head. "See, I was quick. Didn't want to keep you waiting."

She opened the refrigerator and stared inside. "Fuck," she said. "Oh, sorry."

"That's okay."

She bounced over to the overhead cabinets and pulled

out a box. "Ta-da," she said, holding it towards me with two hands. It was a box of Kraft Dinner.

"My favourite," I said. "You have ketchup?"

"Definitely." She opened a drawer and then tossed about twenty little packets of restaurant ketchup on the table.

It seemed to take an awfully long time for the water to boil. Marlene acted a little nervous as she sat back down to sip her coffee. I stared at the tabletop, now feeling strangely awkward around her.

"Here's the thing I need to talk to you about, Nick. I think you are going to have to watch out for Garrett."

"What do you mean?"

"He's going through some kind of change. Have you noticed?"

"Well, maybe. Moody, right?"

"Was he always like that?"

"Never."

"Look, early on he gave me the whole speech, telling me he was in love with me, that I was the most important thing in his life."

I swallowed hard. I was afraid of what she might say next.

"I told him in no uncertain terms it wasn't going to be like that. He had to get that out of his head. I said we could be friends and that was all. He got all mopey, stopped coming to visit for a bit but then showed up one day and said, 'Okay, let's just be friends.'"

"He told me something like that. But I think he still had a thing for you."

"We made the friendship thing work. At least I think we

did. I know people think that is unusual or creepy, but that wasn't it. Your mom even called once, and we had a heart-to-heart. I think in the end she understood."

"My mom's pretty smart about some things. But I just can't imagine you two having that conversation."

"Well, we did. I like your mom. Salt of the earth. But here's the thing. In the last few months, Garrett has been really acting weird. It's like he's got this big chip on his shoulder."

"He just turned seventeen. I think he's worried about what will happen after he graduates this year."

"He had a birthday?"

"Yeah. And he didn't seem so happy about it. Maybe he was expecting a party or something and it was just me and Mom. Pretty lame, huh, for a seventeenth birthday?"

"He didn't mention anything to me about it."

Marlene added the contents of the KD box to the pot on the stove. "It's more than that. I think he's depressed."

"Yeah, he's been pretty down. That's not like him. I mean, he did change in the last year. We used to do stuff together. Goof around, make up games. He doesn't seem to care about that anymore. I just figured he was growing up. Leaving me behind. He sneaks outside at night and smokes a little weed I think."

"Doesn't sound like the Garrett I know. He gave me a lecture more than once about toking up. Sounded like he was the adult, and I was the little punk kid."

"And he hates the job at the Superstore. Tells me people treat him badly. He told me they treat him like shit. He banged his carts into some old fart's SUV and the guy tore into him. Nearly got him fired."

Marlene was stirring the pot of macaroni now, and then set out a couple of plates and forks. She turned off the stove and then scooped something that looked less than appealing onto two plates—a gooey, pale, mucky mass of noodles. "Brunch," she said. "Eat."

I ripped open a couple of ketchup packs and squeezed them out onto the unappetizing KD. In the process, I ended up squirting some on my shirt. "Oh shit," I said.

Marlene grabbed a dishcloth and started rubbing it off, only making it worse.

"Doesn't matter," I said. "No big deal." But then something occurred to me. "Have you told Garrett *anything* about, um, your health issue? About moving?"

"No," she said. "I've been meaning to. I think I told you today as a kind of warm-up. I don't really have a choice. If I want the treatment, I have to go to Vancouver. And I can't keep renting here if I'm gone. So I have to move."

"Do you know people out there?"

"Not really. Not anymore."

"That's all the way on the other coast." A silly obvious thing to say.

"I know."

And the only thing I could think to ask next was, "Are you going to be okay?"

"I don't know," she said. "I really don't know."

12

So brunch consisted of a cold cup of coffee and the worst Kraft Dinner I ever ate. But I ate it all.

Well, almost all. I was down to my last painful forkfuls when Marlene's cell phone rang. She ping-ponged around the kitchen trying to find her purse and then fumbled around in it looking for the phone, eventually dumping its contents onto the kitchen table to find it.

"Hello?" I heard her say. And then it was a series of concerned expressions. Something wasn't right.

I set my fork down and waited to see what was up. I couldn't make out what was being said on the other end.

"I'll bring him right over," she finally said and hung up.

"It was your mother," Marlene said. "Your brother's been arrested. She wants you to go to the police station with her. C'mon, I'll drive you."

Arrested? Garrett? That sounded crazy. I stood up so quickly my chair fell over backwards. Marlene was grabbing her keys from the pile on the table and put a hand on my shoulder as if guiding me to the door.

We walked quickly to her car. It was the same old Honda she had from the first day we met. The door groaned as I opened it and sat down on the seat. Marlene started the engine and backed us out of the driveway in a hurry.

It only took about two minutes, and we were pulling in my driveway at home. My mom was already outside, wearing her old, faded coat and clutching her purse. She was waving for me to join her as she walked to her car, but Marlene rolled down her window and shouted to her. "Come on, get in. I'll drive you there."

My mom just nodded and hurried our way, eyeballed me in the front seat and got in the back. As she sat down, she looked flustered. Marlene already had the car in reverse and was backing up again.

"What happened?" I asked her.

She didn't say anything at first. She put her hand up to stop me from asking more and then leaned over in the seat. I think she was trying not to cry.

Then she took a deep breath and straightened up. "Something at work," she began. "Something in the store parking lot. I think he was pushing a long line of shopping carts back into the store and bumped into somebody. The guy gave him a hard time and started to push Garrett around. Apparently, Garrett hit him with his fist and knocked him down. Someone else in the parking lot called the police."

"I've never seen Garrett hit anyone," I said.

"No, it doesn't sound like him at all," my mom agreed.

"Shit," Marlene said. "Shit, shit, shit."

This silenced my mom and we drove the rest of the way there in dead silence.

~

Things were eerily quiet inside the Halifax police station. I guess there wasn't a lot of crime on a Saturday morning. The three of us stood before a glass window speaking to a man in uniform who seemed to be much more interested in sipping his Tim Hortons coffee than listening to what my mom had to say.

"Oh yeah," he finally said. "The boy with the attitude. You his mother?"

"I said that, didn't I?"

"You did."

"Well?"

He took a long slug of the black coffee, yawned once and got up off his ass. "Let me see what I can find out," he said and walked away.

I don't know who looked more upset—my mom or Marlene. Marlene didn't speak and my mom was shaking. I can't say that anything like this had ever happened in our family.

A woman stormed in through the door and started complaining loudly, to no one in particular, about a parking ticket. A couple of police officers who had entered the waiting room watched her blather, walked right past her and were headed out the door.

But then one of them stopped, gave Marlene the once-over and a hint of a smile crept over his face. It could have been that he recognized her from the club. But he didn't say anything. And then they were out the door.

The angry woman now looked our way and kind of growled. She was damn riled up and gave us looks like we were somehow to blame for her parking ticket.

"Settle down, sweetheart," Marlene said to her. "It's just a frigging parking ticket."

This angered the lady even more and she shot back, "Shut up, bitch."

Marlene just backed right off, but gave us a knowing look.

The woman walked up to the glass window and pounded on the counter, but no one paid her any mind. She pounded a second time and, when no one showed up, she turned and walked out of the room.

My mom was sitting down now wringing her hands. Marlene paced back and forth, and I just stood there with my hands in my pockets.

Then a door opened and the man from behind the glass was leading Garrett into the room.

I'd never seen him look like that before. I don't even have a word to describe him. Angry, yes, but also hurt. But something else as well. Defeated or maybe disgusted. Some kind of weird mishmash of emotions that had transformed my brother into someone I could barely recognize.

My mom jumped up and hugged him to her. Garrett just stood there with his arms to his side.

"He can go," the cop said to my mom. "You'll need to sign some paperwork. But the guy he hit decided not to press any charges when we told him he'd have to appear in court. Maybe you should teach your kid to have a little more respect for his elders," he lectured, which made me wonder how old the guy was who Garrett had whacked.

Soon, we were out of there and back in Marlene's car. "I got fired, too," Garrett announced. "My boss saw what happened. He came out when the cops got there and screamed at me. Said to never set foot on the property again. I guess I really fucked up."

It was the first time he'd ever used the F-word around my mom. I was sitting in the back seat with him and couldn't help but study him and wonder what had become of the brother I once knew so well.

13

Marlene dropped us off, and Garrett didn't say anything to my mom or me. He stormed off to his room and I sat with my mom in the living room, where I watched her fret.

"It's going to be okay," I insisted, even though I was as worried as she was about this new turn for Garrett.

Neither of us saw him much for the rest of the weekend. He went out walking for hours at a time, and when he returned, I was pretty sure he had been drinking or smoking weed or maybe both. I tried to go in his room and talk to him late Sunday night, but he just told me to leave him alone.

So I never had a chance to tell him about Marlene. And the truth is, I was afraid of what might happen when he knew the whole story.

We left the house Monday morning to walk to school as usual, but halfway down the street he stopped. "I'm not going to that shithole today. I'm going to hang out with Marlene."

"Do you think that's a good idea? I mean, we only have a month left and then you're gonna graduate. You don't want to screw it up now."

"What's the point?" he asked.

"What do you mean?"

"I mean, what difference does it make if I graduate or not? It's all fucked."

"What's all fucked?"

"Everything."

"Garrett, just go to school. School sucks, but just hang in there. Finish the damn thing. You're the lucky one. I have to stick it out for a couple more years. I've pissed off just about every teacher in the damn building and they have it in for me, but I'm hanging in there. If only to continue to piss them off."

"You always were—"

But I didn't let him finish. "What? Hopeless?"

"I wasn't going to say that."

"What would you say, then?"

"Obstinate."

"Yeah. That, too."

Suddenly, Garrett looked up at the sky and laughed. "This is kind of funny, you know? You, Nick, you little twerp. You were always the one who got into shit. You were always the one to get in hot water at school, get the lectures, get Mom so worried that you'd end up in real trouble. But now it's me losing my job, getting arrested. Who knows what next?"

"Garrett, don't be a dick. Just come with me to school. Sit in the frigging seat there and get good and bored out of your mind. Take the finals. Walk out of there in a month and do whatever you want."

He looked down from the sky and straight at me. "You don't get it, do you?"

"Don't get what?"

"It's all so pointless."

"Hopeless, you mean."

"Look, don't give me a hard time. That stuff on Saturday —I can't even believe I hit the guy. He was just some old fart that started rattling my chain because I bumped into him with the shopping carts."

"He probably deserved it."

"He probably did. But I went off the deep end."

"Garrett, what the hell is all this anger about?"

"I don't know, Nick."

He punched a fist into the palm of his other hand. "You get out of here. Go to friggin' school. I gotta go talk to Marlene."

"Okay," I finally said. "Skip school, but I'm gonna make sure you're back there tomorrow."

He gave me a sideways sarcastic smile. "Really? You and what army?"

14

You might wonder how someone could get to be the age I was without really having any friends. But that was me.

The answer is easy. I'd always pushed people away. It was like some bizarre kind of anti-social skill I had developed.

It didn't take much to alienate teachers, of course, even the ones who tried to be helpful. The only one who refused to give up was Tasker. He was my so-called academic advisor and the administration had singled him out to try to get hard cases like me "through the system," as they like to say. He'd known me for about a year at that point.

My *modus operandi* at school was simple. For the most part, I just didn't do the work. Most teachers would endure me sitting inattentively in their classes and shrugging if I was called on. But if any of them called me out in class—took me to task for not participating in group work or silly assignments—they would send me to the office, where the vice principal, Mr. Lombardo, would shake his head and say, "Go see your advisor. Let Tasker deal with you."

Tasker's office was more like a glorified closet. Small, stuffy, industrial-looking, no windows at all and with a bookshelf taking up one entire wall, making it seem even smaller. On this day, I ended up there because my math teacher had called me lazy—not exactly an overblown insult. But I had responded by calling Mr. Giles "incompetent."

Well, he was that. He wasn't a very good teacher. But a good student would stick it out with an incompetent teacher, as I'm sure you all have. Most students just put up with the boring shits, skim the textbook, do a minimum amount of work and move on.

But not me.

And maybe if the class hadn't applauded and cheered when I hurled the i-word in Mr. G's direction, that would have been that. But the other students, even the good, dull, ordinary, successful students, verbally supported me in my analysis of the man's pedagogical abilities. And that made things all the worse.

So, there I sat silently in Tasker's little cave, thumbing through a dog-eared copy of *The New Yorker*, looking mainly at the cartoons that I didn't understand, while Tasker finished grading some essays.

When he finally looked up, he said, "What are we going to do with you?" These words had been uttered many times before.

My signature move was to shrug.

Then he leaned forward and took off those steel-rimmed glasses of his. "I'm going to get you through high school if it kills me," he said. And he smiled.

I didn't understand the man at all. I could do or say just about anything in an attempt to piss him off and it never worked. So I had sort of given up on it.

My mom had tried to explain to me that the reason I didn't get along with most men—well, almost all male teachers, at least—was that my chicken-shit father had left when I was so young. I had never "bonded" with a father figure.

I usually didn't pay too much attention to my mother's homespun analysis of why I was the way I was. But the fact that Mr. Tasker *tolerated* me gave him fairly high stature in my books. In the old days, I would have been booted out of school, but not now in these enlightened academic times. And beside my verbal abuse, unlike my brother, I had never actually hit anybody. I'd thrown things, but only at walls and blackboards. Not at people.

Tasker said, "You should not have insulted Mr. Giles in front of the class."

"I know that."

"You got through last week without a single incident. I thought we were really making progress."

"That was delusional on your part." I hated it when he used the word "progress" or hinted in any way that I was "improving" as a student.

"Any particular reason that you broke your cooperative streak today?"

There had been no cooperative streak. If I'd gone a full week without raising shit in school, it had been completely accidental. But because this was Tasker and not just another asshole counsellor or teacher, I gave him an honest answer. "I was worried about my brother."

"What does that have to do with school?"

"Probably nothing at all," I admitted, "but you're the one with the master's degree in education and one in psychology. You tell me."

He pushed his glasses up higher on the bridge of his nose. "Probably something to do with transference. You know what that is, right?"

I groaned. "Don't patronize me, okay? Remember, I told you I read a bunch of old college psych books someone gave me."

"Of course. But I think they might have been a bit out of date. So tell me about your brother."

I sighed, let my eyes wander over the titles on the spines of the books on his shelves for a few seconds and relented. I told him about Garrett. And then I told him about the someone who had given me the books. Marlene.

And while I was doing so, it started to sink deeper into my consciousness. Marlene was sick. And Marlene was leaving. And Garrett was over there right at that minute, getting the double whammy of bad news.

I explained all this to Tasker. Once I had launched into it, it just kind of poured out.

"And exactly who is this Marlene? Some friend of your mother?"

"No," I explained. "She's this exotic dancer who befriended Garrett and me a few years back when we nearly drowned."

"Oh," he said, not batting an eye. "It's good to have friends."

15

I went looking for Garrett at Marlene's right after school. He wasn't there.

Marlene looked really sad and not well. She hugged me to her when I opened the door and held me like that for almost a minute. She told me that Garrett had spent the whole school day with her. She told him about quitting her job, about the tumour in her head and about—moving for good to Vancouver for the treatment and whatever came next.

"And then what happened?" I asked.

She looked quite upset now. "Then he just left."

"What did he say?"

"He didn't say anything. He seemed to understand at first that I have to do this. But then it was like he was mad at me."

"Mad at you?"

She nodded. My stupid brother. Why would he be mad at Marlene? It wasn't her fault she was sick.

I went home after that. My mom was still working, and Garrett was nowhere in sight. He'd taken to wandering off on his own a lot lately and he'd been so moody. And I just didn't know what was going on in his head.

I tried the door to his room, but it was locked—which really didn't mean that much in our house. We only had those interior door locks that you could open by pushing a nail into the little hole.

I'd never, ever broken into my brother's room before, but I needed clues as to what was going on with him. I knew things were bad, though—the mood swings, the anger. But I just didn't know *why* and now this thing with Marlene was going to take him deeper into whatever negative territory he was living in.

Garrett's room was a disaster. Clothes piled on the floor, his bed a big jumble of sheets and blankets. I felt guilty at once for poking around. But I was already there.

Looking around, I wondered how I'd lost him, how I'd lost that great bond we'd had as little kids.

Images of the ice in the Arm kept coming back to me. Images of Garrett coming to save my sorry ass. Images of him getting us ashore. It all seemed unreal and so long ago.

I sat down on his bed and stared into his closet. That's when I saw the vodka bottle. Half empty. It wasn't even hidden. Marlene had given him his first beer. Maybe this is what it led to.

I walked over to his desk and opened a drawer. There was the pipe and a bag of weed. Shit.

I began to wonder if he got the booze and the weed from Marlene. I was pretty sure it was something about her—about our mutual infatuation with the woman—that had made him so moody. But now this.

And now he knew that Marlene would soon be gone. What would this do to him?

It began to sink in that all that time he'd spent with her and the time she'd spent with both of us was just a little too...what? Weird? Creepy? Just not right somehow. While other kids were out playing basketball, skateboarding or just goofing around in the streets, Garrett had been sitting in Marlene's kitchen, listening to her talk about her life and talking to her about his own. Anybody could see that this was just—odd. But was it damaging?

Maybe.

I was sitting down at Garrett's desk, piled high with schoolbooks that looked like they hadn't been touched in a while. When I opened another drawer, I found a spiral-bound notebook like the kind we sometimes use in school.

The cover had been ripped off, and the very first page had the most bizarre sketches I'd ever seen. Demons. Vampires. Zombies. No surprises there. And the artwork was nothing to write home about. But everything looked angry. It was all done in pen, and in places the pen had ripped through the page.

I flipped through and saw violent images of stabbings and shootings. All very crude, some of them scratched out, others framed in a dark red ink.

None of this fit the brother I knew.

I flipped through to some written entries towards the back and saw this:

> Once everything seemed so simple. Everything made sense. Now nothing seems simple and nothing makes sense. Nothing. No one understands me. Well, almost no one. I feel like I don't belong here, but I

have no idea where I belong.

I keep expecting something to change. But it doesn't.

I keep expecting to wake up and everything will be different.

But it isn't.

I don't feel like I fit in anywhere. And never will.

I just don't want to have to feel this way anymore.

None of this made any sense to me. Sure, we had some money issues in our little family. And our dad had split years ago. But we didn't have it as bad as some. I'd had my anger issues and gave people a hard time. But that was me. Not Garrett. What the hell was going on?

I don't know how long he had been standing there, but I heard him cough as I set the notebook down on the pile of junk on his desk.

"What the fuck?" he said in a voice I'd never, ever heard my brother use.

"Garrett…" I began. I wasn't sure what I was going to say next. Say I was sorry, I suppose. *Sorry I broke into your room but…*

It doesn't matter, since he didn't give me a chance to speak. He walked up to me, kicked at the chair I was sitting in and then slammed his fist into my jaw. It knocked me onto the floor, and then he kicked me one in the gut. It knocked the wind out of me.

"Fuck you," he said. "Now get the hell out of my room."

My brother had never hit me in his life. We had played at slap fighting when we were younger, but we both always backed off if it started to go too far. This was different.

I was in shock as I tried to catch my breath. Garrett just sat down on his messy bed and stared at me. There was hatred in his eyes. At least that's what it looked like to me from the angle I was looking at him.

I curled up into a fetal position, I think, still trying to get my lungs to work. Then I inched myself upward, leaning on the wall. Garrett was flat out on his bed now, staring at the ceiling.

I was pretty sure that nothing between my brother and me would ever be the same again. And I wasn't sure I wanted it to be. I really didn't know who the hell he was anymore.

16

I never told my mom what had happened. Nor did Garrett ever apologize. And I didn't forgive him. We weren't talking to each other anymore.

My mom noticed, of course, but when she asked, neither one of us said anything. If she asked more than once, Garrett would just tell her to back off. And she did.

Garrett went back to school and so did I, even though we didn't walk together anymore. We didn't want anything to do with each other and he wasn't around the house much when I was home. He'd come home late, and we could tell he'd been drinking. Or smoking. Or both. He'd stumble into his room and lock the door with a deadbolt he'd bought at the hardware store.

My mom was beside herself with worry and kept asking me if I knew what was going on.

I understood some of it. But not the whole picture.

One Sunday, Mom insisted we all three sit down for a Sunday dinner at noon. Garrett was out walking, and we thought he'd stood us up. But he showed up a half hour late and apologized for that.

I was thinking Mom had some kind of plan she wanted to discuss—something that could dispel the gloom hanging over us all at home.

But it wasn't that at all.

We ate in silence after Mom failed to get any small talk about school going. And then she broke the news. "Marlene called me at work yesterday," she said. "She wanted me to say goodbye for her to both of you. She's gone to Vancouver. She says you both knew she had quit her job and was going back to where she grew up."

Garrett pretended not to react.

I felt like I'd just lost my best friend. Like a light had gone out of my world.

"Did she say if she got scheduled for surgery?" Garrett asked, breaking the silence.

My mom looked puzzled. "Surgery? She didn't say anything about surgery. Is there something wrong? She didn't mention it."

I knew that Marlene and my mom were not close, but it seemed really strange she would tell Garrett and me about something as major as the brain tumour but not explain to my mom why she was moving back out west.

Garrett backpedalled. "It was nothing really. Just something minor," he said. And I wondered why he didn't want to explain the truth about why she had to leave.

And then it hit me. Maybe it wasn't the truth at all.

"Before she left, she dropped off something for both of you."

She left the room and, when she returned, she had two paperback books. She handed the first one to Garrett. *On the Road*, by Jack Kerouac. Garrett stared at it like he really didn't give a rat's ass.

And then she handed the second one to me. It looked like it must have been 600 pages. *The Brothers Karamazov*, by Fyodor Dostoevsky. "She said you'd both understand why."

Why what? I wondered. Why she left? Why these two specific books? Like Garrett had said in his journal, I too now didn't understand much of anything anymore.

We finished the meal in silence, interspersed with my mom making small talk about the crazy customers at Organic Planet.

When Mom was cleaning up the dishes, she threw some car keys down on the table. "Marlene left one more thing. Her old Honda. Said we could keep it. She said that Garrett would be driving soon and maybe he can use it. It's an old rattletrap, but she signed it over, so I guess it's ours."

Garrett stared at the car keys on the table. I was pretty sure I knew what he was thinking.

And it scared me. It really did.

17

With Marlene gone, I think Garrett had lost the only anchor in his life that was holding him in place.

I'd always been adrift, so I missed her presence, but my life still chugged along more or less the same as it always had. Trouble at school—mostly of my own doing. But occasionally teachers that I'd really pissed off blamed me for other stuff I didn't do. Once lunkheads like Jonesy Will and Bart Fleming noticed this, they'd set me up for more academic crime and punishment. I had racked up accusations of verbal assault, theft, and obscene postings on Facebook about teachers, staff and students. And then there were the usual misdemeanours that actually were of my own doing: cheating on tests, plagiarism and disrupting classes with what I thought were hilarious comments.

Tasker was advising me through this dark phase of my life in which I felt abandoned by Marlene and now Garrett, whose presence at home was more like having a moody ghost for a brother than a real person. I talked to Tasker about Garrett since I didn't have anyone else to talk to. "You can talk to me about anything," he had said more than once. "It's strictly between us."

The guy was a die-hard do-gooder who took all the shit I

threw at him and acted like it was no big deal. He claimed it was because he was a Buddhist, but I had a sneaky suspicion that, beneath his usually-calm exterior, he had some grand plan that, in his own way, he hoped to eventually "break" me and turn me into a model citizen.

Well, that was never going to happen, but he was my only ally of sorts in an otherwise uncaring and hostile world, so even though I would never admit it to him, he was probably the best friend I had. Well, the *only* friend I had. Or maybe he just thought he was doing his job as the king caregiver of lost causes.

Garrett had been avoiding hanging out in the house at all lately. Sometimes he'd be asleep in Marlene's car in the driveway. When he didn't show up in the house, Mom or I would walk out with a flashlight and peer in through the windows of the car. And there he'd be, curled up in a fetal position in the backseat.

He'd look like he was dead, so Mom would open the car door in a panic and check. Garrett would wake up and be in a really rotten mood so they'd argue out there in the driveway—or at least Garrett would shout at her and the neighbours would turn on their porch lights and peer out to see what the trouble was.

But me, I could tell that he was just conked out. I'd hold my breath and put my ear up to the window and could hear his familiar snore. I'd know my brother's snore anywhere. Even though we hadn't shared a room since we were little kids, I could always wake in the middle of the night, hear him gently snoring from across the hall, and it comforted me.

However, now he was sleeping outside in the car on some nights and that wasn't quite the same. I could see that dog-eared copy of *On the Road* was sometimes on the front seat if the moonlight was shining in through the windows. Sometimes I'd stand there, listen to the snoring if the neighbourhood was quiet enough, stare at the moon and just wonder if Garrett would even go back to being my big brother again.

He'd show up at school some days, but not others. Mom and I had both given up on the lectures to "just hang in there for another month until exams are over." He'd always done well in school. Up until this year. Now he was throwing it away.

I started to blame Marlene. I mean, maybe she and Garrett had something more going than I could see. Maybe it had gone beyond the puppy dog infatuation. Maybe the decline and fall of my good brother was all her fault. Hadn't she given him his first beer? Didn't the house reek of marijuana sometimes? I'd never seen them once touch each other, but who knows?

I had settled for something Marlene had said to both of us one soggy Saturday morning in March. "Most people don't quite get it. There are so many kinds of relationships other than boy-girl let's-get-married. We've mucked it up so badly that a man and a woman can't have a life-long friendship without being labelled something else. Or a woman and a woman. We're all locked into stupid patterns and role models that our grandparents set down. They look modern but they're not.

"You want to see the damage?" she said. "Just look at the

mugs on some of those lonely sad cases sitting at the bar where I work. Then tell me we haven't completely made a mess of this whole relationship thing."

I knew for sure I'd not be able to see those lonely sad cases or their mugs, but I knew she had a point, and it was one she felt strongly about. And it did help explain—or at least I thought it did—why she befriended Garrett and me.

~

And so the days rolled on as we headed into warmer weather. I carried *The Brothers Karamazov* around in my backpack, but it was huge—hundreds of pages. The cover was ugly, and it looked like a stupid book.

But I was sitting on a bench down by the stream in the park one day, with the sun out and the squirrels chattering and me worrying about Garrett, my mom and all her worries and my own sad state of affairs. That was getting really depressing, so I finally cracked open the book and read this on the first page:

> He was only twenty, his brother Ivan was in his twenty-fourth year at the time, while their elder brother Dmitri was twenty-seven. First of all, I must explain that this young man, Alyosha, was not a fanatic, and, in my opinion at least, was not even a mystic. I may as well give my full opinion from the beginning. He was simply an early lover of humanity, and that he adopted the monastic life was simply because at that time it struck him, so to say, as the ideal

escape for his soul struggling from the darkness of worldly wickedness to the light of love.

No shit, I thought. *This makes no sense.* So I read the passage a second time. If the whole book was like that, I'd never get through it in a million years. And why should I even bother to read it anyway? I never read most of the stuff they assigned in school.

But I almost always read the stuff Marlene had given me to read. So I read the passage a third time.

God. The stupid names. Ivan? Dmitri? Alyosha? Are you kidding?

Right about then, one of those big squirrels had come down from an oak tree and stood at my feet. I guessed he was used to people in the park feeding him. I held out my hand and he sniffed but, realizing I had nothing for him, he scampered off. I turned back to the passage in the book.

Did Marlene think that this Russian lunatic Dostoevsky would somehow unlock some secrets of the human mind for me, some truth about our most difficult existence?

Well, maybe. That would be just like her.

Was I supposed to identify with one of the brothers? If so, who was I then? Alyosha? And if that was the case, then Garrett must be Ivan. But we didn't have a Dmitri.

Still, why had Marlene given me this dense, difficult, ridiculously huge novel to read? The woman was probably just messing with my head.

I closed the book again, but something there stuck in my brain: *his soul struggling from the darkness of worldly wickedness to the light of love.*

There was probably nothing more to it all than Marlene giving me one of her cast-off books before she left for Vancouver. But the words in that phrase haunted the hell out of me. *Soul struggling? Darkness of worldly wickedness, light of love.* Jesus.

I didn't read another word. I took a deep breath, listened to the squirrel chatter above my head and watched the sunlight filter in through the new leaves of the tree.

18

Marlene's car now sat on the grass alongside our cracked and crumbling concrete driveway. Garrett would sometimes go out there and just sit for hours at a time. He claimed he liked the quiet and that he was doing schoolwork, but I doubt that was often the case. Now that it was warmer, he had taken to sleeping out there every night in an old musty sleeping bag he'd had since he was a kid.

It made my mom pretty nervous, but she kept saying it was "a phase he's going through."

To be honest, I felt like I had lost a brother and I wanted to know how and why. So I went out there one morning after a restless night when I couldn't sleep. The dew was still on the grass and birds were singing as the sun was just creeping up over the trees.

The car doors were unlocked, and I opened the door and sat down in the driver's seat.

Garrett was curled up in the backseat, half in and half out of the sleeping bag. I didn't see any booze bottles or smell any weed. In fact, the car smelled like Marlene.

Garrett didn't even wake up when I closed the door. So I sat there for a quiet minute with my hands on the steering wheel.

Marlene had given the keys to the car to my mom, but we both knew where they were. She had said the car was for Garrett. But Garrett didn't have his driver's license yet and he didn't seem that interested in preparing himself for it. And that was part of the problem. Garrett didn't seem to be interested in much of anything.

There was a small statue of Buddha mounted on the dashboard, right alongside of one of those silly little plastic Hawaiian dolls that jiggled and danced from the motion of the car. Hanging from the rear-view mirror was a small, delicate metal cross on a fine silver chain. I could almost feel Marlene's presence in the car, and it was comforting. Maybe that's why Garrett wanted to sleep out here.

I leaned back to get a good look at Garrett, but I accidentally tapped the car horn.

He sat bolt upright and lurched forward, ready to lay a fist into whatever stranger had entered his little domain. But I caught the fist with my own hand and looked him straight in the eye.

"Nick, you little dweeb. What are you doing out here?"

"Checking on my big brother, asshole," I said.

He flopped back down. "For Chrissake."

"Garrett, what's with you? What is...this?"

He lay on his back now, staring up at the ceiling. "This?"

"You. Everything. What?"

"I don't have to answer to you," he grunted.

"Yes, you do."

"No I don't."

It was one of those really dumb back-and-forth ping-pong conversations that brothers would have when they were little kids. But I had usually been the pissy one in any of those conversations. Now it was different.

"There's an old Chinese proverb that states that if someone saves your life, you are obliged to look out for that person from then onward."

"I thought Marlene said it was the other way around."

"Well, she got it wrong."

"So now you're the big expert on Chinese proverbs? Well, guess what, we're not old and we're not Chinese."

"Well, guess what? It doesn't matter. You are my responsibility because you saved my ass on the ice that day and, in fact, you saved my ass plenty of other times."

"Kid's stuff. Nothing more."

"But I need to know. What happened?"

"What do you mean what happened?"

"What happened to you?"

"Oh, not this shit again. Did Mom ask you to come out here and harass me on that?"

"No. I came out here to harass you all on my own."

"Bug off. Let me go back to sleep."

"I'm not leaving until you tell me what's going on with you. Is this all about Marlene leaving? You weren't really in love with her, were you?"

Garrett pulled the sleeping bag up over his head. He didn't say anything at first but then he shocked me by giving a muffled answer. "Well, I was, sort of. At first. But so were you, you little creep."

I didn't say anything to that.

"But I got over that," Garrett said, poking his head out. "It was sort of ridiculous. But I always felt a bit more alive after talking with her. I think she understood who I was even when I didn't know. She had a way of explaining things. The world made a little more sense when she was part of it."

"And now she's gone," I added.

"Worse than that," he said. "She's got this brain thing. I read up about it. It's awful."

"But she said it might be that other thing…something not so bad, something benign."

Garrett shook his head. "No, she told me before she left. She'd had a few more tests. They confirmed she has a brain tumour. The worst kind. She's probably into the treatment now. Radiation. Chemo. If that doesn't work, she'll have to have an operation. She didn't want to tell you. She told me to keep it to myself. But there. Now you know."

"It sounds bad."

"It is. When she left here, she said she was moving in with an old friend from university. They were both dancers when they were going to school. Jessica, I think her name was. Someone to help her see this thing through. But I read about the odds. Not good. It all sounds hopeless to me."

There was that word. "That's what everyone used to say about me."

"And you deserved it, you little twerp. But this is different. This is bad."

"Garrett, there's nothing you can do about it. Why are you beating yourself up and doing all this weird shit?"

He sat back up. "I don't know, little brother. It's like nothing much makes sense to me. It's not just Marlene. I just don't seem to see much point to anything."

"So now it all seems hopeless?"

"I don't feel like I belong here anymore. I don't know if I belong anywhere."

19

Garrett gave me a look that said he wanted to be left alone. So I got out of the car and went back into the house, feeling even worse than before.

His final words echoed in my head. That was exactly how I had felt most of my life. Aside from having a good mom and a brother who was always looking out for me, once I left our property, it always seemed like I didn't fit in anywhere. Like there was no purpose to any of the stuff everyone else was doing.

I went into my bedroom and tried reading *The Brothers Karamazov* again, half expecting some kind of revelation, some clue left behind by Marlene to guide me. But I couldn't concentrate on the long paragraphs and impossible names and the sheer number of Russian characters.

In reference to the father of the brothers was this line, however, in the very first paragraph of the book:

> He was all his life one of the most senseless, fantastical fellows in the whole district.

I could tell it was meant to be an insult, but it was the "fantastical" part that caught my attention. And I wondered if such a thing related to my own father, who I hardly ever knew at all. My mother had often referred to him as having been a person prone to living in a "fantasy world."

Even though he had abandoned us, she rarely said much of anything negative about him, if she spoke of him at all. He had deserted us, leaving for a "better life," part of that fantasy thing he might have shared with the man in the book with the ridiculous name of Alexey Fyodorovitch Karamazov.

Truth is, I hardly ever thought about him myself. I'd seen pictures and maybe I had some distant foggy memory from when I was a baby, and he was still around. And maybe me being more or less fatherless made me the way I was—a misfit in the world. But in many ways, I liked being me, even if I was a pain in the ass to pretty much everyone at school and was a loner to boot, with no real friends.

Such were the thoughts going through my brain when my mother knocked on my bedroom door and came into the room. She looked at the book I was reading, and it clearly puzzled her. But she knew better than to ask me questions about why I was ever doing whatever I was doing. She knew I didn't like it.

"Can I come in?"

"Sure."

She was holding something in her hand. An envelope. "This came in the mail this week." Her voice sounded sort of funny. I think I understood.

It was a letter. No one ever mailed us a letter. A Christmas card maybe (one a year from dear old Dad out west), but not a letter.

"Can I see it?" I asked, curious about such an archaic artifact.

I held it in my hand. The envelope was blue, and it was square. It had a stamp with a picture of the Queen. The handwriting on the front was exquisite—loopy, feminine letters. It was addressed to Garrett. It was postmarked from Vancouver. It was from Marlene.

"What should I do with it?" she asked, sitting down on a corner of my chaotic bed. "Garrett seems so, um, fragile these days. I'm afraid that—"

I cut her off. "No, you have to give it to him." I flipped it over and over in my hands.

"Shouldn't I read it first? Just in case it's bad news. I can steam it open with the kettle and close it back up and give it to him if it is okay."

My mom, the super spy. This was so unlike her, spooking around something personal. So totally unlike her. But she was worried about Garrett. And so was I.

Truth was, *I* wanted to read the letter. I wanted to read it before Garrett. But I said, "No, you have to give it to him."

She nodded and reached out for it, but I pulled it away. "Let me," I said.

I suddenly didn't trust her. Despite what I just said about her not being sneaky, I knew she'd do just about anything to protect both of us from something harmful. Even lie to us.

"Okay."

So I walked it right out to the Honda.

Garrett was just sitting in the back seat, staring out the window like a weirdo. I opened the driver's door again and plopped back down into the seat. "You got a letter," I said, handing it to him.

He looked at for a second or two before it registered and then he slid his index finger along the back flap and opened it. The paper inside was blue as well. There were at least three folded pages, and the words were on the front and back of each page.

I sat there gripping the steering wheel and didn't look at Garrett as he read. The car was quiet except for his breathing and the sound of him turning over the pages. I tried to fathom why she would have written a letter and sent it through the mail. She knew we were bad with emails and didn't have cell phones, but Mom had a phone, and I was pretty sure Marlene knew the number. She could have just called and talked to Garrett. But this was different.

I waited for Garrett to finish reading. I could see my mom staring out at us from the kitchen window. She was watching as he opened the back door of the car and got out. He threw the letter down on the cracked concrete, said, "Fuck," and walked off down the street.

I didn't go after him. I knew better than that.

20

I got out of the car and scooped up all three pages of the letter, and the envelope, before the breeze had a chance to
scatter them. My mom was already out of the house and
walking towards me.

"What was in it?" she was asking even before she made it
down the steps.

"I don't know," I said, but I was clutching it tightly and
headed into the house with my mom now right beside me,
wringing her hands.

I sat down at the kitchen table and held the first page in
my hands to read with my mother hovering over my
shoulder.

> Dear Garrett,
>
> I know you'll find it strange to receive a letter like
> this, but I have a lot I need to say and this just feels
> like the right way to do it.
>
> So, first, let me tell you I am doing okay.
>
> And then, I need to tell you I am in treatment. Still
> in the hospital. It was not benign. It was the "real
> deal" as they say. So the radiation treatments were
> not what I expected. Things got pretty intense. And

there was chemo, like we talked about. I've got good people working for me.

I was going to send you a photo but decided that it would make me look worse than I actually am. Sure, I've lost my hair and I'm pale as a ghost...but they say that's normal. Although I don't know what is normal anymore. I wear a scarf that Jessica gave me, and I like it very much. But I don't wear it all the time because I don't leave the hospital. They say I'm too vulnerable to any germ I might pick up out there.

They keep me isolated but that doesn't matter much. I don't have any visitors except for Jessica. You'll remember that I don't have any real family out here. My foster parents from long ago have moved on somewhere up north. And this is just as well. Aside from Jessica, I guess I must do this thing on my own.

And, I don't know why, but I really want to tell you about Jessica. I mentioned her to you before, but you may not remember. We were best friends from all the way back to high school. We went to UBC together, got our first jobs dancing together. We were very close. She was the one who decided eventually that things in our relationship were moving too fast. She broke things off and that's when I moved down east. Start a new life, make some new friends. Make a go of it.

And I guess I did. You know about the job. I'm not bragging about it, but at least I could support myself. The friend thing was a bit tough. All the men were wrong and the women I danced with were in a different place in their lives.

And then you and Nick came along. Best friends I ever had.

Except for Jessica maybe.

So, when I came back here, guess who was there waiting for me?

She was. And she's been here every step of the way. Every day. Even though I now look like the bride of Frankenstein, she says she loves me. And I believe it. This woman is helping me get through it. And she'll be there until…well, whatever, whenever.

I must have stopped reading then, at "whenever." My mother took the page from me and reread that last paragraph.

"There's more," I said, turning to the next page.

But I didn't continue since my mom grabbed it from me, which was completely unlike her. She began to read it out loud.

Despite all the treatment and the kind people here and, well, everything, the doctors in charge say they will need to operate to remove the tumour which is still there. They are just waiting for my permission.

So far, I haven't said yes. Jessica says it's the thing to do, but she doesn't want to push my decision. The doctors say that it is the only way but that it is risky. Of course.

And maybe, Garrett, this is why I am writing to

you. I have time to decide, they said. The radiation and chemo have bought me some time, as they say. So I didn't want to rush into it. But I'm scared, Garrett. And I remember so well you and I talking about being afraid. You said you weren't afraid of anything. I knew it was not just the young man talking the talk. I knew you meant it.

When we first met, I asked you about drifting out to sea and how you knew you had to get you and Nick back to shore. And you said you were never afraid. I didn't believe you at first. You put it this way. "I just did what I had to do." And never thought twice.

And we talked about fear after that. Well, my fears anyway. Always a little afraid at work. All those staring men. I pretended not to show it, but it was there. And fear of growing old. Growing old alone. And you said I'd never be alone. You always said nice things to me. And I always appreciated that.

I remember that you never once admitted being afraid of anything and I still think that was just a pose. But then you admitted you were afraid for Nick. That he'd never get past his anger, he'd never fit in. And you were afraid there wasn't anything you could do about it.

But that wasn't real fear. That was caring.

So, I guess I was hoping I could tap into whatever was in *your* head that day out on the water when you knew that you had to do the thing you needed to do. With no fear at all.

And I don't even think I expect you to write back to me about this because you may not be able to explain it any better than that. You'll only say it was just the thing you had to do. No thinking whatsoever. But the bottom line is that I already feel a bit better about what will come next by just writing these words to you, knowing you will read them, knowing you will think about me.

And that somehow gives me a bit of courage...if that's the right word.

And I know that the whole thing with Jessica may not be what you expected from me and, frankly, I'm a bit surprised. Maybe it shows that when you hit a rough patch in your life, you never know who will show up to be there for you. To help out.

Like you, and Nick too, I suppose. You two frozen wet scoundrels showed up in my life just when I needed...something.

So I'll end by thanking you for that, Garrett. Thanks for being there.

Sorry I had to leave. Sorry I can't offer you some more insight into how to live your life. I hope the car is running okay and that you get your license soon. Keep an eye on your little brother and be kind to your mother.

Love,
Marlene

21

When Garrett came back, he didn't say a word to us and went right into his room. We'd learned in recent weeks not to ask him any questions when he was like this. Just leave him alone and let him stew.

But this time was different. The letter from Marlene would be sitting heavy on his mind.

He did come out of his room for dinner and, while dishing out the spaghetti, my mom cautiously approached the subject. "The letter?" she asked.

Garrett just twirled some spaghetti around on his fork. "It made me sad, but there's nothing I can do about what she's going through. I'm not even sure why she wrote it."

"I think she wanted you to know that you are important to her," my mom said. "That's all."

Garrett shook his head. "Yeah, maybe. But I kind of wish she didn't send it. It's just one more thing that seems hopeless."

There was that word again.

"What do you mean?" my mom asked.

"Never mind," Garrett said. "Let's change the subject."

We sat in silence for the rest of the meal.

After that Garrett retreated to his room. I knocked on his door around nine o'clock and walked in as he was stashing something under his bed.

"Wanna talk?" I asked. "Like the old days."

"What old days?"

"When we were young."

"That was then. This is now."

Which was that annoying answer that Garrett had used on me before.

"Do you miss Marlene?"

"That's a stupid question. She's gone. What's the point?"

"Just wondering."

I had a million things I wanted to say to him. I wanted to talk to him about missing school, about how he needed to just hang in there and go through the motions. To finish the last few weeks of school and get his diploma before he blew it all away. Mom and I had already said this many times, but I knew that nothing more I could say would be the magic bullet that would bring him back to his old self.

As I was leaving his room, he gave me a look that I couldn't decipher. Then he held up what looked like an imaginary glass towards the ceiling in some kind of toast. "Here's to the old days."

I mimicked his toast. "The old days," I echoed.

~

In the morning, I awoke to the sound of my mom crying.

I raced to Garrett's room. He was gone. When I ran to the front door and looked out, I saw that the car was gone, too.

22

"I should never have accepted that car," my mom said, wiping tears from her eyes. "I figured it would just sit there until Garrett got his driver's license. But now this."

I stayed there with her for most of the morning, making her tea and just saying everything would be fine. But that wasn't what I was feeling.

I knew Garrett could drive a car. Mom had let him drive a couple of times, hoping it would light a fire under him and he'd take the driver's ed course and then the driver's test. But Garrett showed little interest in that direction. It was like everything else in his life since he'd changed. He just didn't seem to care at all.

"Maybe we should call the police."

"No," I insisted. "Definitely not. Look, he's seventeen. He went off somewhere on his own. He's not a missing person, and if you send the Mounties looking for that Honda with Garrett behind the wheel and no license, he'd be in deep shit."

My mom gave me a dirty look. Funny that, even at a time like this, one simple word could offend her.

So we sat there. Helpless. Waiting. For what, neither of us was sure. But whatever it was, it wasn't going to be good.

Sometime shortly before noon, Mom's cell phone rang. She answered. I could hear a male voice on the other end, but not the words.

"Oh, my God," she finally said. "Where?"

I held my breath until she hung up.

"The Mounties stopped him at the New Brunswick border," she said, and then took a deep gulp of air. "We need to go there right away."

"Is he okay?"

"I think so. But they're holding him until we get there. We need to go now."

~

My mom drove well over the speed limit the whole way there, something I'd never seen her do in my entire life.

And then we arrived, and were standing in the waiting room of yet another police station. My brother the criminal.

The woman in uniform who listened to what my mom had to say was exceedingly polite. "We established that the car was not stolen," she said. "But your son was driving without a license."

"I understand," my mom said. "Can he go home now?"

She slid a piece of paper across the counter. "Here's the official charges. But look, he's seventeen. It's on him, not you."

My mom looked at the paper and read as the woman in uniform waited patiently. "Can we just pay the fine?"

"Yes."

"Do you take Visa?"

"We do."

About ten minutes later, Garrett was led into the room. He looked more defeated than ever.

They impounded Marlene's car. They said they would call the owner and ask what she wanted done with it. Even though Marlene had signed the document turning the car over to Garrett, he had never officially registered the ownership change with the province.

My mom reluctantly gave them Marlene's cell phone number. I wondered what she would be thinking when she heard about Garrett's rash decisions. One more thing for her to worry about.

Garrett was sullen and unapologetic. My mom was fuming. She kept her cool at the Mountie headquarters but once we were in the car, she slammed the palm of her hand into the steering wheel. "Fuck, fuck, fuck," she cursed in a kind of throaty whisper. I'd never heard her use the word before. Ever.

The sky was ashen as we left the town of Sackville, New Brunswick, and drove across the Tantramar Marsh. There was a cold wind whipping this way and that and transport trucks seemed to want to bully us off the road. I was up front, and Garrett was in the back like he was now our prisoner, not the Mounties'.

As we climbed in elevation, heading up to the Cobequid Pass, it started to snow. Yes, snow. It was near the end of May, but here it was snowing—big fat shitty wet flakes that were accumulating on the highway and making it slippery. I watched as my mom gritted her teeth and tightened her grip on the steering wheel. The drive had become a true white-knuckle event.

Just before we got to the toll booth near the high point of the mountain pass, she pulled off the road onto the shoulder, shut off the car, slammed her fist into the steering wheel once again and got out into the blustery, wet snowstorm without a coat on.

When we both heard her let out a long, nearly inhuman, scream, we cringed. Garrett slid down into a fetal position and I didn't move at first.

But when Mom just stood there staring up into the blizzardy sky with her hands clutched to her face it was too much. I got out and walked over to her.

There could have been tears on her face, or maybe it was only the big, wet, melting snowflakes. I thought she might scream again from that look, but instead she grabbed me and pulled me towards her like a rag doll and squeezed so hard I couldn't breathe.

I walked her back to the car, where she sat down behind the wheel and pulled herself together. "We'll talk about this when we get home," she said.

I nodded but Garrett didn't move.

Right after that, as we pulled up to the toll booth, an old guy who looked like somebody's grandfather refused to take my mom's money for the toll. He just nodded a knowing, soft smile and waved us through. He'd been watching.

23

When we got home, she sat us both down at the kitchen table. If we are told to sit at the kitchen table and there is no food involved, that's a worrisome omen.

"Sit," she told us both, and grabbed onto Garrett's sleeve when he tried to keep walking towards his room. "We need to get your father involved in this," she said out of the blue. "But first I need to tell you something."

Garrett was giving me a look now. A look that said, *What the fuck?*

Mom poured herself a drink from a bottle of brandy that had been gathering dust in a high kitchen shelf since I could remember. I was thinking that she was really losing it. This was so unlike her.

But she sipped it, grimaced and began. "You had another brother."

Garrett's jaw dropped. I felt this big fog moving into my head. What on earth was she saying?

"He was born a bit less than two years before Garrett came into the world." She wasn't looking at us but at a photograph of the rocks at Peggy's Cove that was on the wall. "Your father and I were very much in love back then. The baby was a blessing. We named him David."

She drained what was left in the glass. "He seemed perfectly healthy, and we loved him very much. And then, when he was only a month old, something happened. He died in his sleep. It's more common than most people believe. Sudden Infant Death Syndrome. SIDS. It was horrible. Couldn't have been much worse. I went off the deep end. Your father took it even worse.

"Although they explained to us over and over that it wasn't anything we did and there probably was nothing we could have done to prevent it, we blamed ourselves. And then we kind of turned on each other. I blamed him and he blamed me. We'd lost David and there was nothing to console us.

"But we stayed together, got some counselling. At first it seemed to help, but then it didn't seem to help at all. Like other couples before us, we believed that if we had another child, we could get past it."

She looked at the bottle, now sitting on the table, and I thought she'd take another drink, but instead she slid it away. "So along comes Garrett. And for a while, things got better. We were never the same, but we soldiered on. I was home with Garrett, Russell was working—spending more and more time at work and less at home. It wasn't perfect, but it was better. Do you remember much about your father, Garrett?"

Garrett shook his head. "Not much. But some. I was always happy to see him, but it was mostly you raising me. It was okay, though. I remember being happy."

"And you were. A few years later, we were still trying to make things work, Russell and I, and so we decided to have another child. You, Nicholas. So Garrett had a little brother that he loved, but sometimes resented, as older siblings do."

She turned to me. "But you were, well, more difficult. Stubborn from the start. Smart as a whip but dancing to your own beat. By two, you had a word for everything and every circumstance. And that word was *No*. I loved you as much as Garrett...and David. And so did Russell. But we had only covered up our old wounds and they started to show much more now. The chaos of home life with two little boys seemed to be too much for him. He started to drift away. We stopped communicating."

"And then he was gone," Garrett said, finishing the story. "I remember coming inside from playing out back and you were crying. The car was gone. He was gone. And he never came back."

My mom touched the side of her face and then rubbed her hands together. "He went about as far away from us as he could and still be in Canada. He sent some money at first, but then it just stopped. He found another woman. Well, the first of several. He had a new life. He called once in a while to ask how things were. I told him we were fine. He told me how great life was for him in his new life. He was selling real estate in a very hot market. I could tell he'd really found his calling."

"But he wasn't willing to share some of the money he made, was he?" Garrett asked.

"I told him we didn't need it. I think at that point, I just wanted him out of my life. He asked about you kids and I'd tell him all was fine. He never mentioned David, though. Even before he'd left, he'd stopped talking about that and if

I brought it up, he'd change the subject."

"Why didn't you tell us about David?" I asked.

"I figured you didn't need to know."

"But I thought he left because of me," I said.

"If it wasn't you, he would have found something else. The death of a child, they say, is something that some parents can't recover from."

"Yeah, but he just stopped being a parent," Garrett asserted. "He stopped being our father."

Mom attempted a smile. "Hey, I did okay, right? *We* did okay."

I was going to say, *Until now*. But I didn't.

She turned to Garrett. "This thing you're going through, what is it you want?"

Garrett splayed out his fingers and shook his head. He had that look. That hopeless look. He probably didn't really have the words to say it or even a real understanding of what he was going through.

"So, we're going to call your father and see what he says we should do," my mom said.

"Screw that," Garrett snapped.

My mom didn't like that. She'd always had a thing about language, but now we were in totally new territory. She slammed down her empty glass on the tabletop and pointed a threatening finger at Garrett. "So, tell me this. Where were you headed?"

Garrett didn't answer. Which had been his answer to everything in recent weeks.

"And you did make it all the way out of the province, didn't you?"

"Just barely," he said.

"Well, you know your father lives out there."

"So?" Garrett blurted.

"So maybe it's time you go give him a visit. And he can bloody well pay for his son's airfare. You're not going to drive. And if the bastard says no, I'll tell him I'm going to go out there and I'll find a way to wreck his perfect little life."

I'd never seen my mom so fired up. But I wasn't sure this made any sense. Why send Garrett off to a father who didn't want to have anything to do with his son? Or his sons. "What are you talking about?" I asked, incredulous.

My mother screwed the top off the brandy bottle now and poured herself another drink. "Nicholas, are you willing to go, too, so you can keep an eye on your wayward brother? It seems he needs someone to look out for him. And you seem like the only candidate."

"Hell yeah," I answered.

"Good," she said. "So there."

24

It took my mom some digging through a kitchen drawer to find her little book of phone numbers. But then in a flash she was on her cell phone, punching in the one she needed.

Miraculously, she got an answer. "Russell, it's me. I need to talk to you about our boys."

Her boys sat at the kitchen table and watched her empty the brown liquid in her glass yet again. Watched the determined expression on her face and listened to her speech that sounded like she'd been rehearsing it for years.

We could detect small bursts of protest coming through the phone from the other coast. Small attempts at explaining reasons why the proposal was a bad idea. But there was a determination and a fierceness in her voice that was like an unrelenting army.

My mother, the boss.

We could only follow the conversation from what we heard Mom saying.

"They're your sons."

"Yes, you need to pay for the flights."

"You have a new girlfriend who doesn't like kids? Great. That makes this all the better. She needs to make some adjustments. And so do you."

"Yes, e-transfer. Today, please. I want to see them on that flight by the weekend."

"Thank you." Click.

"It's all set," she said to us. "He'll pick you up at the airport in Vancouver. Two days from now. It's a long flight with a stopover in Toronto, probably. I'll have to pack you some sandwiches."

It was the weirdest thing, but nobody said a word about missing school. And not a word had been uttered about Marlene. And I'm sure Garrett had as many questions as me, but he said nothing. There was a hint of a smile on his face as my mother screwed the cap down tight on the bottle and put it away in the cabinet.

Holy shit.

Garrett and I were going to the West Coast. I was soon to be reintroduced to a father I hardly ever knew. But my head was still whirling round, thinking about a brother I never knew existed.

When I got to my room and saw that book lying on my bed, I remembered there were three brothers in *The Brothers Karamazov*. I had found the novel almost unreadable and had given up on it. But the three brothers thing spooked me. Had my mom opened up to Marlene at some point about the loss of David?

No, wait. Actually there were *four* brothers in the story. Dmitri, Alyosha, Ivan and the illegitimate son, Christian, who was never really accepted as part of the family.

But that connection was way too weird to even contemplate.

~

We'd never been on a plane before. Never. Not even once. It was a completely new world to us.

My mom had second thoughts and almost called it off, but one look from Garrett told her we had to do it.

Air Canada to Toronto, then a layover when we walked around the enormous terminal. And then the long flight to Vancouver. High in the sky, west across the Prairies, over the Rockies and down into a foggy world.

I had not really explained what was up to Tasker, back at school. It was his job to keep tabs on me. But I usually kept him in the dark. He'd owned up to the fact that the principal had assigned him to personally get me through this year, whatever it took. Keep me moving through the grades and get me out the door as soon as possible. But now I'd skipped out on school and skipped out on him. And I had no idea what would happen to Garrett in terms of graduating.

And here I was, standing with my big brother in another big, crowded airport. We were watching the luggage spill out of a doorway, riding a revolving conveyor belt. To me, it was like something out of a movie.

We were waiting for our one battered suitcase, and it was a long time coming.

A guy in uniform had a German shepherd dog up walking the conveyor belt now, stepping right over the luggage as the dog sniffed his way alongside. I silently prayed that Garrett had not stashed any weed in our suitcase. Even though it was legal, he and I were still underage. And I wasn't sure if you were allowed to carry it on planes. I also hoped he hadn't brought any of the other drugs I worried that he'd been experimenting with.

But soon we had the suitcase and were shuffling between the other travellers toward the exit from the arrivals gate.

"Hey, Garrett, Nicholas. Over here," I heard a man yell.

That would be us. But I didn't recognize him.

This man. Our father. Absent these many years. Tall, slightly bald, a bit puffy around the waist. He was wearing what looked like an expensive suit and, as he waved, he lifted a pair of sunglasses up onto his head.

I'd seen photos of him before, but I didn't know this man. He could have been an imposter for all I knew, trying to abduct us. But then why would anyone want to do that?

Garrett steered me towards him. He was all smiles. I had this feeling I'd not just flown across the continent, but that I'd been dropped on another planet.

As we approached, I realized he was not alone. He was with an Asian woman, much younger than him, and a little kid. What the hell?

"Oh my god, you guys are big," was the first thing he said to us as we approached. "I wasn't expecting...," he began and then paused. "I don't know what I was expecting."

I could have said a thousand things just then. Words I'd imagined in my sleep, even practised out loud sometimes. *You stupid piece of shit. You ran off. You abandoned us. You asshole.*

But in recent weeks, I'd become good at *not* saying the first thing that came to my mind. Tasker had said that it was a sign of maturity, and I had told him most impolitely to go fuck himself.

Our father touched Garrett on the shoulder but not me. He looked at me and something in the way I stared at him made him look away quickly and clear his throat.

He nodded towards his companions. "This is Chen," he said. "And her son, Pin."

I think Garrett and I both just stared at the poor little kid. He was maybe only six years old, skinny as a toothpick, and I thought maybe that's why they called him Pin.

Chen saw the look on our faces, I guess, because she piped up, "And no, I don't dislike children. I don't know why your father said that on the phone." She elbowed my dear father in the ribs, and he looked somewhat embarrassed.

I could have explained why he said it. He didn't want us here.

"Let's get you guys out of here and get us all home," Dad said.

Home. That was the word he used.

His car was in the parking garage. It was a big, black SUV like the CIA men drove on the TV shows.

Once he was planted behind the wheel and pulling out of the garage onto the highway, he started chattering about what else? All about himself. "I moved from selling homes into commercial real estate," he said. "The market is boom-ing. I'm making a killing at this game."

We were in the backseat, with Pin sitting between us. Garrett looked over the kid's head and stuck two fingers in his mouth, pretending to gag. Pin looked up and saw this. The kid lit up with a big smile.

"I'm glad you two could come out to visit. I have a lot I want to show you."

"Dad," Garrett asked. "Um, did Mom tell you exactly why we're here?"

"To reconnect with your old man, of course."

Garrett rolled his eyes. "Yes, of course," he said sarcastically. "But there's something else."

"Something about a friend in the hospital out here you wanted to visit."

"Yes, that."

"We'll get you settled in, and you can go there tomorrow," Dad said.

Garrett looked steamed. "I want to go there now," he insisted.

Our father said nothing but looked straight ahead. Chen whispered something to him.

He was shaking his head no but then Chen turned around in her seat and said, "Before I moved Pin and myself here from Hong Kong, my mother was very ill. I visited her every day in the hospital. Things were getting very bad in Hong Kong with the new rules, and I wanted us to leave, but I couldn't leave her behind. But when she left us, Pin and I came here."

"I'm sorry for your loss," Garrett said, sounding so different from that angry hopeless teenager of recent times.

Pin took a small video game out of his pocket and handed it to me. He touched the screen and it lit up. "Cool," I said and went to hand it back.

"No, keep it. Maybe you can play it with your friend in the hospital."

It seemed like the most unlikely thing I could imagine us doing with Marlene, but I suddenly liked this kid. Liked him a lot.

Garrett told my father, "Vancouver General Hospital."

"VGH," Chen echoed. She took out her phone and I think she was looking up directions.

"VGH it is," Dad said.

I put Pin's little video game into my jacket pocket, and he looked very pleased.

25

My dad pulled up to the entrance of the hospital. It was huge, simply enormous.

The reality of being here and visiting Marlene was suddenly catching up with me, and I found that I was scared. Frightened of what we might discover once we found her.

"You sure you guys don't want to get settled with us first and then come back?" my father asked.

"No. We're here," Garrett insisted. He already had his hand on the car door. In a split second it was open, and he was standing outside.

My father looked a bit confused. "Jesus," he said.

He fumbled in his pockets, handed me a card. "Here's our address." Then he pulled out his wallet and handed me a fifty-dollar bill.

I'd never seen a fifty-dollar bill in my life.

My own confusion seemed to prompt him to lift a second one out and hand it to me. "Take a cab. We'll be waiting for you."

I tucked the money into my jacket pocket with the video game, and got out. It was only then that it really sunk in. My father lived with Chen and her son. My mom had called her his girlfriend, but they were obviously in a more permanent relationship, he and this woman from Hong Kong. And why did I feel like she was more on our side than he was?

Garrett tugged me towards the towering hospital. It was so much larger than anything I expected, and I was trying to get my head around the fact that it was filled with sick people. How could they have so many sick people out here in Vancouver? And somewhere inside this vast complex was Marlene.

I watched as my father's black SUV pulled away and suddenly felt totally disoriented. Garrett was walking towards the entrance marked EMERGENCY and I had to stop him and explain that we should use another door. He realized I was right, and we hurried to the main entrance.

Inside, it was crowded, and I spotted the information desk before Garrett did. We had to wait in line and Garrett kept rubbing his knuckles on the palm of his hand— nervous energy emanating from him.

When it was our turn, he explained who we were looking for. The woman tapped some keys into her computer. She told him the room number, but I couldn't hear her. Then she said, "Take the third elevator on the left."

Garrett charged ahead and I followed him to the third elevator. When the door opened to the Oncology floor he rushed out and I was right behind. He went one way and then another and then began to run down the hall, drawing some unwanted attention to us as I tried to catch up.

The door to the room he was looking for was closed but he didn't knock. He just went in. I followed closely behind and gently closed the door behind me.

A woman was reading a magazine and we clearly startled

her. "What are you doing?" she whispered in a frantic voice. "Who are you?"

But Garrett didn't answer. He was looking at Marlene, lying in the hospital bed with a tube up her nose and bandages around her head. At first, I thought maybe we had the wrong room. She was unrecognizable.

Garrett stood there frozen.

"Get out," the woman with the magazine said.

"This is Garrett. I'm Nicholas," I said, as if that would explain everything. It must have taken a few seconds for it to sink in.

"How did you get here?"

"We came to see Marlene," I said.

The woman's expression changed. She took a deep breath. "She told me about you. I'm Jessica."

"How is she?" Garrett asked, approaching the bed cautiously.

"She's weak. But she came through the operation. It's been a few days. She's just sleeping now. Please don't do anything to wake her."

Garrett took a step back. "Operation? What about the chemo? The radiation?"

"It helped. But it wasn't enough."

"Is she gonna be okay?" he asked.

Jessica gave a sad soft smile. "I don't know."

Garrett looked away from her. He looked straight at me. The anger had returned. Damn. Why that of all things? Why here? Why now?

"Who does know, then? Who the fuck can tell us something?"

Jessica looked defiant now. "Get out!" she insisted, trying not to raise her voice. "Don't come back until you can act civil."

Garrett let out something that sounded like a guttural growl, turned, opened the door and walked out.

I stayed behind. "He doesn't mean to act like that. I'm sorry. Marlene means a lot to him. To us. But I think Garrett was in love with her. I know that sounds weird, but maybe it's why we're here."

She gave me a sad soft smile again. "She's easy to fall in love with. I love her, too. We've known each other since high school. When she found out she was sick, she decided to come home to me."

26

So, by this point in the story, Mr. Tasker will understand why I disappeared from school. Yes, disappeared. It's turning into one hell of a sob story, so he'll probably just throw up his hands and tell the administration to pass me for the year and forget about the fact that I didn't come back to classes, exams or any of that stupid shit that goes with the end of yet another dreadful school year.

But there's more to tell, and now that I'm this far into it, I guess I'll have to finish the whole damn thing.

And yes, it all seemed bloody hopeless.

Don't get me wrong. I had no problems with the fact that Marlene and Jessica had a thing going. I always knew Marlene was different. But don't misunderstand that, either. I mean different like me. Like she was not what most people thought she was. She travelled her own road. She had her own way of looking at the world. She was just trying to be who she really wanted to be.

Just like me.

Only no one even had a label for me. Except, well, you know. Hopeless.

And I really liked Jessica. I wanted the two of them to have a Hollywood ending. Happily ever after.

But there I was, over 4,000 kilometres from home. On the far side of the continent. I just reunited with my asshole father after many, many years. He had a girlfriend and a kid. Not his kid. But a kid. They lived together.

Did that make Pin my half-brother? Or was it step-brother? Sort of.

The fourth Karamazov? No? A bit too weird. What the Russian writer would have labelled the bastard brother. But we didn't use that word anymore, except as an insult you hurl at someone who pissed you off.

I could have used the word about Garrett, however, at that point. Why the hell was he acting like this? Letting his anger out at a moment like that. I wanted to find him and punch him.

But what if I walked out into the hall and he was gone? Like *gone* gone. It wouldn't have surprised me.

"I'll be right back," I told Jessica.

"Maybe it would be better if you left, too," she said, but in that soft voice of hers.

I needed to do *something* right then. My brother had freaked out. He was not there to guide me anymore. I felt this powerful need to connect with Jessica, to let her know I was here for support… even though I didn't really have a clue as to what form that would take.

So I walked over to where she was sitting by the window. At first, she just sat there and looked at me. But then she got it. She stood up. I gave her a hug.

When I pulled back, she was wide-eyed, shocked. I didn't know what to say.

"I needed that," she finally said. "Go get your brother. Tell him not to act so stupid."

When I went out into the hall, Garrett was nowhere in sight. I asked an orderly if they'd seen anyone come out of the room.

The guy pointed down the hall. "I think I saw him go into the bathroom."

And that's where he was. When I walked in, I could hear someone sobbing inside one of the cubicles. I'd never head my brother sob in my life.

"Garrett, Jessica wants you to go back in the room. You need to pull yourself together. C'mon, bro, we came all this way to see Marlene. Gotta do this thing."

"Fuck off," he said.

"Where am I going to fuck off too?"

"Go find Dad and tell him I'm not going to his house."

"Dad? Since when did you start calling him Dad?"

"I told you to fuck off."

"We gotta go back in there."

"We don't have to do anything. Leave me alone."

"If you don't come out, I'm coming in."

I don't know why, but I started thinking about various movie scenes that took place in men's bathrooms. Men having conversations at the urinals. Some bad guy beating the shit out of the good guy and busting his head on a sink or a toilet. That sort of thing.

Seconds passed. No sobs. But no brother unlatching the door.

"Fuck it," I said out loud.

Then I had to decide, over or under. Over seemed problematic. I wasn't much of a climber. But under? This was a hospital after all, and I was in the bathroom trying to get into a toilet stall.

I grabbed the top of the stall door. I hoisted myself up. It was much harder than I anticipated.

Garrett was smacking my fingers that were in a death grip on the metal.

I pulled myself up, got a leg over the other side. Then the other leg.

He was hitting me now. Not hard. But hitting.

And then I was down. Garrett was standing now. We were face to face. Brother to brother. Two Nova Scotian boys in a toilet stall in a Vancouver hospital. Jesus.

"Let's go back in," I insisted.

"She's dying," he said. "It's not fair. It's not supposed to be this way."

"We don't know if she's dying. Look, what did we come out here for?"

"I don't know. I wanted to see her. I wanted to see that she was okay. I thought everything would go back to normal for me then."

It was a nice little fantasy. I wouldn't have thought Garrett would have fallen for it. But he must have conjured it up in his imagination when Mom wangled us those tickets to fly out here.

"Do you remember what Marlene said the first time we met her?"

Garrett was pulling himself together now. He was breathing hard. "No, I don't," he said, as he steadied himself by leaning back and accidentally hitting the metal lever that flushed the toilet. "What did she say?"

"She said, 'Take off your clothes. Both of you.'"

A hint of something. Not quite a smile. But something. "She did, didn't she?"

"And then she added, 'Kick your shoes off, dammit.'"

"We were wet and freezing."

"Yes, we were."

I reached behind me with one hand and snapped the door latch loose.

"Everything made so much more sense back then," Garrett said.

27

A couple of young men in green scrubs gave us a weird look as we emerged from the toilet stall. I shrugged and Garrett followed me as we walked back out into the hallway.

"We're gonna go back in there and do this, right?" I said.

"We are."

I opened the door and Jessica was standing over Marlene in the bed. She gave us a questioning look.

"I'm sorry for acting like an idiot," Garrett said.

She said nothing, put her finger to her lips and then pointed down.

Marlene was awake. Her eyes were wide open. Jessica motioned for us to come forward.

I hung back as Garrett inched forward, a bit unsteadily. He stood beside Jessica and leaned over.

I watched as Marlene lifted her hand up and touched his face. She said nothing at first and let her hand linger there. I couldn't make out her first words but there was a hint of something. Not quite a smile, but something that came over her face.

Jessica reached for a remote that sat on the table and elevated the top part of the bed ever so slightly.

I would not have recognized Marlene.

She had that tube running into her nose. Her face was pale and puffy, her head wrapped in a bandage. And she had bluish marks under her eyes. It was the look of someone who had gone through a battle. And it reminded me that she had been battling for her life. From the look of her, the battle was not over.

"It's a reunion," Jessica said in her soft, kind voice. "Let's celebrate."

"I don't have any beer," Marlene said, her voice a scratchy whisper that she struggled to get out.

Garrett smiled a real smile then. And I felt like I really did have my old brother back.

Marlene blinked a few times and then her eyes began to close. She whispered something else to Garrett and, as he leaned over to listen, he gently kissed her on the cheek.

As he stood back up straight, Jessica touched the remote and the bed lowered itself as Marlene fell back asleep.

"Thank you. Thank you both," Jessica said. "Will you come back tomorrow?"

"We will," Garrett said.

That was our cue to leave.

Walking down the hall, we passed the two young men in scrubs who clearly remembered us from the bathroom. It must have been the fact that they didn't look away that prompted me to reach down and grab Garrett's hand. I expected him to flinch and pull it back, but he didn't.

Two brothers walking down that hallway in far-off Vancouver, holding hands like two little boys.

"What do we do now?" I asked.

"Go hang out with our idiot father, I guess."

"He never really was much of a father," I said.

"He was at first," Garrett said. "I still have some good memories of him. But then everything changed."

"When I came along, you mean?"

"I don't think it was just you. I think it was him."

"What do you mean?"

"People change. Even fathers. Mom tried to explain it. Maybe something about that older brother neither of us knew about."

"Why didn't she tell us about him before?"

"Too painful, maybe. I don't know."

"But she didn't run away. From us."

"No, she didn't. Even though you were a little brat right from the beginning." There was no animosity in his voice, and I knew he was speaking the truth.

"Was I that bad?"

"Yes. I remember."

"Bad enough to make our father run off and never come back?"

"Apparently so."

Of course, it was my father who had coined my nickname and it had stuck. I don't remember it, naturally, but that was the story around the dinner table for the three of us.

"But let's not call him Dad," Garrett asserted now. "He doesn't deserve it."

"Then let's just call him by his first name. Russell."

"Okay. But do we like him at all, or is he just trying to help us out of guilt?"

"I don't know if we like him," I admitted. "And, yes, he's doing this out of guilt."

"Let's work it," Garrett said.

~

Outside, it was really the first time I noticed that it was warmer than back in Nova Scotia. The sky was blue, though, now, just like back home. But it all felt different. Different but the same. Because I could smell the sea. It was mixed in with all the smells of the city. But it was there.

I took out the business card Russell had given me. "Guess we can take a cab with the loot he gave me."

"I'd rather walk," Garrett said.

"Okay. Which way?"

Garrett took the business card and stared at it. Then he spotted an old scruffy man with a sleeping bag wrapped around him, sitting at the base of the tall hospital building. I followed Garrett as he walked over to him.

"Hey, buddy, can you tell me where Simpson Avenue is?"

He looked a little stunned and seemed surprised that anyone was talking to him. I could see he was sitting on a piece of cardboard and had an empty bottle tucked into the sleeping bag.

He thought about the question for a few seconds, bewildered at first but then began to point and give directions. When he finished, he repeated part of what he had just said and then asked, "You got that, or do you want me to draw you a map?"

"No," Garrett said, "I think I got it."

"It's a long walk," the old guy said.

"It's a good day for a long walk," Garrett said gently.

"It is that."

"Thank you."

Garrett started off in the direction he had been pointed, but the old guy reached out. "Son," he said, "do you have any change you can spare?"

Garrett took out his wallet and gave him the five dollars he had left after buying a sandwich on the plane. Then he looked at me.

I shrugged at first but then took out one of the fifty-dollar bills. I handed it to Garrett. He had no idea how I'd come into the money. But without asking, he handed it over to the old man, then turned back to me with a big question on his face.

I felt like I didn't need to explain. Instead, I handed the man the other fifty.

He seemed a little stunned at first but nodded. "I thank you kindly, son. Now have a good day, eh?"

28

It was a mighty long walk to Simpson Avenue, in a part of the city called Point Grey. My father had specifically called his neighbourhood *West* Point Grey. Once we got past the traffic and found a bit of shoreline where we could walk alongside of the bay, it became less of a chore and more fun.

I was thinking that whatever body of water this was. It was my first look at the Pacific Ocean and I felt a small thrill dance through me. There were some windsurfers on the water, and we passed a canoe rental place where a young couple was putting on floater jackets.

We had been walking in silence for a long while when I finally asked him the big question. "Do you think she's going to die?"

He shoved me hard on the shoulder so that I stumbled off the path. "She's not going to die. So shut up."

"Of course. Sorry."

My brother still had the anger in him. But we were here. I was going to see this through with him. That's all there was to it. We'd be back there to the hospital tomorrow and the day after that. However long it took.

We had to stop a few times to ask for more directions. Garrett had retreated to whatever fog was inhabiting his brain.

One old gent explained that we were now in a part of town called Kitsilano and the body of water was English Bay. We just needed to keep walking along the shoreline west and then turn inland when we got to a place called Jericho Beach. I liked the sound of that.

Dad's house—Russell's house—was big. It had light-coloured bricks on the outside and was located in a pricey neighbourhood. I guess the real estate business really had been good.

Pin answered the door when we rang. He seemed happy to see us.

Then Chen showed up and welcomed us in. "Come on in. Your father is on the phone. He'll be down soon. Let me show you where you'll be staying."

The place was like something out of a magazine. She led us down a flight of stairs and past a large rec room with exercise equipment and two big-screen TVs.

Our bedroom looked like it was out of a showroom, and it appeared so new that I don't think anyone had ever slept in there before. Our one old battered suitcase sat on a chair.

"Thanks," I said as Garrett threw himself down on one of the beds, looking beyond exhausted.

"I'll just leave you two to settle in for a bit," Chen said.

~

I guess this is the part where I should tell you a bit about Russell. Well, for me, he didn't make a good first impression. I'll say that for starters. Although I guess it wasn't really a *first* impression. He had been there for a few years after I had been born. He was the one who labelled me Hopeless, as you might recall. And it stuck. He hung around long enough to do that and...well, long enough to make us all feel like crap when he left.

But now here we were. And here *he* was. I felt like we were from two entirely different worlds.

Garrett and I had both fallen asleep in our clothes on top of the beds when he knocked and asked to come in. He sat down in an armchair by yet another big screen TV. "Your friend, how was she?"

Garrett took a deep breath and leaned on his elbow. "She was just great," he said sarcastically. "She said she felt a whole lot better after the brain tumour was removed."

My father looked puzzled.

"No she didn't," I countered. "She's recovering. She was glad to see us."

"No doubt," he said.

He seemed at a loss as to what to say next.

Garrett was sitting up now and looking our father over, sizing him up. "So, this is your life now, Russell?" he began. "Can I call you Russell?"

"Sure," he said. "Don't want to call me Dad?"

"Let's just stick with Russell."

"Okay."

"I know you were kind enough to pay our way out here and now you're putting us up, but do you mind if I ask you some questions?"

Russell folded his hands in front of him as if giving Garrett his full attention. "Shoot."

"Okay. For starters, what were you thinking when you left us back in Nova Scotia all those years ago?"

It looked like he had been expecting this. "I'll be honest with you. I was thinking that I needed to start over. I was thinking I had made a mistake—marrying too young, trying to raise a family. I wasn't cut out for it."

"We know about David," I interjected. "We thought that had something to do with it."

He nodded and looked me directly in the eye. That was the first time I noticed that he looked a lot like Garrett. Not me. But Garrett. "That shook us both up. Your mother and me. Shook us up badly. We worked hard to cover it up. To pretend it didn't happen."

"But it did happen," Garrett asserted. "And I understand that a parent doesn't get over that sort of thing easily."

"We should have gone for more counselling. But we didn't. We put it behind us...although it never really went away. We just didn't talk about it. And then you came along."

"You seemed like a pretty good father, from what I remember," Garrett said, shocking me.

"Thanks. I appreciate you saying that, considering..." His voice trailed off, but then he picked up the thread. "Your mother and I both pretended that all was well. I wasn't happy with my job—but who was in those days? Just starting out in real estate. In Nova Scotia, God help me. Nobody was buying. I knew I was missing out there and could have done better just about anywhere else."

"But I think Mom was still hurting even after I came along," Garrett said. "Once I was old enough to really see her as more than just my mom, I could tell. There was a sadness there she was trying to cover up."

"There was that," Russell said. "And we both thought another child would make all the difference."

"Only it didn't," I interjected. "It made things worse. I made things worse."

Russell threw up his hands. "It wasn't your fault."

I had to pause and think about what he just said. Yeah, it was my fault. Only I was too young to be responsible. Just a baby. Just a rotten little kid who didn't know much of anything. And as I got older, I understood some of what had happened. And I did feel guilty. "But you just left and walked away."

"I felt that life was passing me by. I convinced myself that if I moved out here, if I got myself established and worked my ass off, that everything would turn around. I would move all of you out here with me and we'd all be better off."

"But it didn't play out that way, did it?" Garrett countered.

"No, it didn't."

"Why?"

"I met someone."

"Chen?"

"No, it was long before that."

"So that changed everything?" Garrett made it sound like a question when it was more of a statement.

"I told your mother about it. I was only trying to be honest." It was such a bullshit line.

"And?"

"And she said she never wanted to speak to me again. I said I'd start sending money. And I did. I mailed her cheques. But she never cashed them."

"Guilt money?" Garrett had fully taken over the interrogation now.

"Of course."

"And then what?"

"And then we stopped communicating."

"And that was the end of that?"

"Until now," he said. "Now my two boys are here and I'm getting to know them finally."

"You are so full of shit, Russell," Garrett snapped. "So full of it."

29

Russell was already gone first thing in the morning when we got up. Chen was getting Pin ready for school and offered to make us breakfast.

Garrett just shrugged but I was starving. "Please," I said.

She made us a big pancake breakfast as she finished getting Pin's lunch packed and asked him a string of questions. *Teeth brushed? Homework? Cell phone? Asthma puffer?*

Garrett didn't say anything, but he ate as ravenously as I did.

"You're a good cook," I told Chen. I was thinking she was a pretty good mother, too, but didn't want to overdo it. As I was finishing, I was wondering what our own mother was doing back home and if she was worried about us. If she was, in fact, doing okay on her own.

When he was finished, Garrett just got up and waltzed back to his room, but I offered to help wash the dishes.

"Just put them in the dishwasher," Chen said.

We'd never had a dishwasher. I looked around and saw it but couldn't figure out how to open the door. Chen had to help.

"Your brother, okay?" she asked.

"It's hard to tell these days. I think it's good we came out, but I'm still worried about him. He's going through a phase." That was my mother's term when she was trying to put a good spin on the nosedive Garrett had taken. I knew it wasn't just Marlene and I knew it wasn't just a phase. Garrett was in a dark place; all I could do was be there for him.

"Where'd Russell go?" I asked.

She seemed to think it was funny that I called him by his first name. Garrett had told me to call him that and nothing else. Except Asshole, of course, and I wasn't about to use that term around Chen. Garrett's current term for him was *The* Asshole. Which I surmised made each of us Son of Asshole Numbers One and Two.

"Your father had some important meetings today."

"Real estate stuff? Selling houses, right?"

"Well, he's not exactly a real estate salesman anymore. He buys and sells properties. Properties that he owns."

"Oh. Big tycoon, right?"

"Something like that. He seems to know what he's doing. Very successful."

I was just thinking how funny it was that he was so successful, while back in Nova Scotia my mom was scrounging to do all she could just for us to get by.

"When my mom called, he said you didn't like kids and that was why we shouldn't come out here."

Chen looked embarrassed. "I don't know why he said that."

I had the explanation for that. It was because my father was a certified card-carrying asshole. But I didn't say it.

"Pin looks like a happy kid."

"He is. Sometimes they give him a hard time at school,

though."

"Because he's Chinese?"

"I think so. But he doesn't like to talk about it."

"I used to get picked on at school. I know what it feels like."

"Why'd they pick on you?"

I realized it was a little harder to explain. "The teachers would say it was because I couldn't keep my mouth shut. I always had something to say to someone and, generally, it wasn't flattering."

"Why would you do that?"

"I don't know. I just did."

Chen opened the dishwasher again, put in some kind of powder, closed the door and turned it on. Weird to say, but it was the first time in my life I'd ever seen anyone do that.

Chen noticed that I seemed fascinated. "What did you do when the other kids gave you a hard time?"

"I asked Garrett to punch their lights out."

She seemed shocked. "And did he?"

"Usually."

The kitchen got quiet for a minute and then Chen sat down at the kitchen table with me. She had a really nice smile. I had wanted to hate her from the moment we arrived, but I had to admit to myself I liked her.

"Garrett's close to finishing high school, right?" she asked.

"He should be there right now. Exams coming up. It's his last year. I'm afraid he's going to blow it."

Chen shook her head. "I know that it's important that he's here. For your friend. And to get to know his father, too.

I'm sure Russell can work something out. Garrett can make up the work. Take GED tests maybe. He won't lose it if he's willing to explain the whole story."

"Maybe."

"But, Nicholas, I think there's a better option for him."

"What do you mean?"

"I'm not sure I'm supposed to speak of this, but Russell was talking about asking Garrett if he wants to stay here with us. He thinks that if he introduced your brother to the business he is in, there would be a place for him. A really good opportunity he might not find back home."

It was a bomb exploding in my head. Garrett staying here? What about me?

"It would be a whole new life for him, a head start on a good career."

I didn't know if I would laugh or cry. Not once had Garrett ever talked about "a career." Maybe when he was little and wanted to be an astronaut or a demolitions expert or a mountain climber but not lately. But where did I fit into this grand plan?

I guess she was reading my mind because she said, "You'd have to go home to Nova Scotia to be with your mother and to finish your own years of school. But maybe Garrett would lay the groundwork and you could come out here when you finished high school as well."

Lay the groundwork? What was that supposed to mean? I had a million things to say to her then, but all I said was, "Thanks for the breakfast. It was really good. I gotta get Garrett so we can get back to the hospital."

"I'll drive you," she said.

30

It was a quiet drive to Vancouver General and the traffic was bad. Chen had the sunroof open on her Mercedes and the air coming in from above was warm and smelled of flowers or apple blossoms or something.

Chen offered to park and come in with us, but Garrett shook his head. "No. Just us."

So she dropped us off at the front door and I did my best to keep up with Garrett as he marched at an almost frantic pace down the hall and up the stairwell this time to Marlene's floor.

Jessica was still sitting in the room, reading a hardback book without a dust jacket. Marlene was sitting up, looking much more alert than when we had first arrived. She smiled as we walked into the room.

Amazingly, Garrett smiled as well. A big, healthy smile I hadn't seen in a long time. He walked right to her, leaned over and whispered something in her ear that made Marlene close her eyes and then open them with a kind of flutter.

"The dynamic duo returns," she said.

"How do you feel?" Garrett asked, like every other fool who ever walks into a hospital to visit.

"Like I've been run over by a bus," Marlene said, but she was smiling.

"Just tell me who the driver is, and I'll kick his ass," Garrett said, sounding like the big brother I once knew.

"Didn't I teach you anything about nonviolence?"

"You did," Garrett shot back. "I faithfully read those books, as you asked. Thoreau, Gandhi, Martin Luther King, Nelson Mandela."

"No kicking ass then."

"Well, okay."

It was silliness, but it was good to hear.

Jessica put her book down as I walked over towards her. I was just trying to find a spot by the window where I could feel the sunlight and be out of the way. "What are you reading?" I asked.

"Just something I picked up at a bookstore yesterday," she almost whispered, setting the book beneath the chair. "Elisabeth Kübler-Ross. You're probably not familiar with her."

"No," I said. "Me, I'm trying to wade my way through *The Brothers Karamazov*."

Jessica looked puzzled. "Why on earth would you be reading that?"

I nodded towards Marlene, who was watching us. I think she almost laughed but the effort must have caused her pain. I could see it in her face.

Jessica turned towards her. "You unloaded all your old dusty books on these boys before you left? What was it, some kind of punishment?"

"A challenge," Marlene said. "Nicholas has the same first

name as the last czar of Russia, so I thought he needed to read Dostoevsky. And especially *Karamazov*. It's about brothers."

"And how are you liking it so far?" Jessica asked.

"It's hard to read. Long sentences. Difficult words. Too many characters with long strange names."

"But you're reading it?" Jessica asked me. "You haven't given up?"

"I am."

"Why?"

"Because Marlene asked me to read it."

"So there," Marlene said. "I had my reasons."

"What about that one?" Jessica asked, pointing at Garrett. Garrett piped up. "*On the Road*."

"Jesus," Jessica said. "Really?"

"Garrett has a restless spirit. It suits him."

"Is that true?" Jessica asked Garrett. "Do you have a restless spirit?"

He looked a little embarrassed. "If Marlene says so."

A nurse walked in the room then and began fussing around. She first looked at the chart hanging from the bed. Then she checked the drip from the IV bag and examined the bandages on Marlene's head. She didn't even say anything; just gave a curious look at this odd little crowd of visitors, and then left.

When she was gone, Marlene coughed a bit, cleared her throat and began what seemed to be some kind of speech. "So here's the thing," she said as Jessica put her hands together and a worried look crept over her face. "They say the operation went, and I quote, 'fairly well,' but that there may still be some of the tumour left. My doctor keeps telling me how lucky I am, but look at me. I don't feel that lucky."

"Don't be silly," Jessica interrupted, but Marlene immediately shushed her.

"Could be more radiation. That would be a whole lot of fun." There was sarcasm in her voice, but tinged with humour. "Or possibly more surgery, but not 'til I'm more healed up. And that, of course, would make me the life of the party."

She paused, took a breath and then added, "I could always say no to any of that, just sit here for months and get bedsores while watching old *Seinfeld* reruns. Life, as they say, is not always a bowl of cherries."

Jessica was rolling her eyes now. Or was she on the verge of crying?

"Or I could insist that I go home and just see what happens."

Garrett didn't like the sound of that. "But you want to be cured, right?"

I'd heard a phrase before in an old song. *The sound of silence.* I don't think I knew what that sound truly was until that moment.

"There is no cure," Marlene said bluntly.

"But I thought you said the operation went well." Garrett said.

"As well as can be expected."

Jessica was standing by the bed now. "I know this is all a bit new to you, but we've been living with it for a while now. Listening to what the doctors have to say and reading everything we could. Marlene is right. There really is no cure. It's a matter of extending life expectancy."

"It's a bit of a cliché," Marlene added as Jessica put a gently hand on her forehead. "But we're all going to die. It's just a matter of when."

Garrett was losing it, I could tell. "Then, don't be stupid, Marlene. Do the radiation. Let them do the next operation. You want to live, right?"

Jessica laid her head on Marlene's chest and closed her eyes. Marlene seemed to be looking at Garrett with pity in her eyes. "Yes," she said. "Of course I want to live."

"Then don't say shit like that," Garrett concluded.

Marlene backed off from speaking about her situation any further. "That's what I always like about you, Garrett. You always tell it like it is. No bullshit. I've missed having you around."

"Well, I'm here now," he said, almost defiantly.

31

When it was time for us to leave, Garrett insisted that he wanted to stay. But Jessica walked him out into the hallway and read him the riot act. I had a few quiet minutes sitting with Marlene as she faded off to sleep.

Looking at her, I had a feeling deep down that she wasn't going to make it. I tried to force the thought away, but it hung over me as a very dark cloud. I'd never had anyone close to me die before and it seemed impossible that Marlene could. Her spirit had been so strong. Now she looked tired and weak.

Maybe I was wrong. I prayed I was wrong. And I don't think I had ever prayed before in my life.

The door opened then. "C'mon, little brother, we have to go."

I tried not to look at the people in the hallways on the way out. It was just too depressing. Old men and women in wheelchairs. Younger ones as well—being wheeled down the hall with trolleys holding up clear IV fluid. And the family members and staff wheeling them. No smiles here. Nobody was having a good time. I wanted to run and just get out of there.

Garrett had a determined look on his face.

Once we were out into the grey Vancouver daylight, I asked him, "What are you thinking?"

"I'm thinking we should get her the fuck out of there."

"Don't be stupid. She needs to stay there if she wants to live."

"Yeah, but that's just it. Jessica just told me. She doesn't want to live. Not like that, anyway."

"What are you talking about?"

"Don't you get it? It's terminal. One way or the other, if she stays there, she's going to die."

"But if she stays with the treatment, she'll live longer."

"You call that living?"

I didn't have anything to say to that.

"She talked to Jessica about having some control on when it would be over."

"Control?"

"She wants to be able to call the shots if she feels her time has come."

"No way. That's just crazy talk."

"Well, Jessica is opposed to it. She's been trying to talk Marlene out of it. And she's there, watching things. 24/7. Jessica says she won't have any part of it."

"Just crazy talk is all it is."

"Yeah, crazy talk."

Garrett was walking at a fast clip. His mind was working overtime, I could tell, and that worried me. But I could see he had shaken off the zombie in him.

Everything was different out here in BC. None of this was going as expected. All the old rules seemed to have changed. More than ever, though, I was feeling adrift, at sea. Helpless? You bet. Hopeless? Yet again.

I wanted to be more than just the little brother following whatever Garrett did, watching out for him, but not being able to do a damn thing about anything. And what if he took up our father's offer to live out here for good? I had to go home. To Mom, yes. But to what else? A shit school and a shit life.

We were down by the water again. It was as grey as the sky now. I could see why they called it Point Grey out there. Grey people living grey lives. Probably all of them rich assholes.

~

When we got to the house, Russell was waiting for us. He had a big grin on his face. Opposite of us.

"Why the grumpy looking mugs?" he asked.

"Don't want to talk about it," Garrett said.

No one else seemed to be in the house. "I wanna take you for a ride. Gonna celebrate."

Garrett gave him a look that could fry meat.

"Celebrate what?" I asked gloomily.

"Closed a deal today. An entire condo. Thirty per cent profit. Never had one that worked so well. The market is just—over the top. They came in at well over the asking price."

Yep. That was our dear old dad. Real estate tycoon of some sort, I guess. Pleased as could be with his wheeling and dealing. Sounded like easy money. Sounded like an entirely different galaxy from the one we had been living in with Mom always scraping to get by.

Did he ever even think of us, while his real estate star was ascending into asshole heaven?

Garrett was about to say something nasty. I elbowed him. I didn't want to mess up the status quo. We were here, weren't we? A roof over our heads, a place to sleep and no daytime rules to keep us from visiting Marlene.

"So let's celebrate," I said without an ounce of enthusiasm.

"Great," he said, pretending not to notice the tone. "I wanna take you guys to the beach. We'll take the Porsche."

I hadn't seen any Porsche. I couldn't believe the man had three fancy-ass cars, while Mom was driving an old wreck back in Nova Scotia. Chen had a Mercedes and Russell had been driving that black SUV, brand new from the looks of it. So this was his little macho sports buggy.

The car had been in the garage, and it looked like it had just come out of some car dealer's show room. A convertible with the top already down. "A 911," Russell said, opening a fridge in the garage and taking out a six-pack of something. Beer?

"Craft beer," he said as if to answer me. "Buy local, ya know? Only because this is such a special day, though, and I want to share it with you two. Don't tell your mother."

Right. Like he would care what she thought about it.

I was pretty sure Garrett was about to spit in his face, but he was looking at the cans. I guess he really wanted some beer because, when Russell opened the driver's door and sat down behind the wheel, Garrett followed him and sat shotgun. That left me to squeeze in behind them, into a really tight backseat that didn't seem designed for anyone to actually sit in.

"Put your seat belts on," Russell said with a little smile. Only I couldn't see any seat belts in the backseat anywhere and Garrett just ignored him and looked straight ahead.

The garage door opened, and we backed out into the driveway just as the sun started to come out. The car had a throaty roar and Russell gave it the gas as soon as we were out onto the street.

About ten minutes later we passed a university with hundreds of students walking about on a beautiful campus. "UBC," he said. "Best damn university in Canada."

Like one of us would ever go there, I thought. But I couldn't help but stare at the crowd of students who all looked so happy and carefree.

Then he was pulling into a parking spot by a forest and jumping out of the car with the six-pack dangling from his hand. "C'mon. We're here."

"Where's here?" I asked.

"Wreck Beach," he said. "I love this place. Just don't pay any attention to the weirdos. It can't be helped. Price you gotta pay to live on the West Coast."

He led us down a steep path through a forest of the most gigantic trees I'd ever seen. I was in awe.

West Coast was right. All the rules were different here. I had to watch where I stepped to avoid squishing some kind of large black slugs the size of my fist. But the forest was amazing.

Garrett must have had his mind on the beer, because he was going right along. No complaints whatsoever.

When we emerged from the forest, the sun was out in full. The beach was wide and beautiful, with a few large rocks here and there and massive logs that must have floated in from somewhere. There were university students hiking along with backpacks and people sunbathing.

But there were also some people here and there just walking around naked. What the hell?

Russell saw the look on my face. "Like I said, don't pay any attention to the weirdos. This is Wreck Beach. Some like to think it's a place you can just take off your clothes. Not my cup of tea, but to each their own. Like I say, price you gotta pay. Just ignore them."

Easier said than done. It was hard to ignore the bare-ass people as they walked right past us as nonchalant as they could be. It wouldn't have been so bad if it wasn't for the fact that they were mostly old and flabby or skinny and sunburnt.

Russell didn't seem to pay them any mind at all as he led us to one of those logs on the beach, sat down on the sand in front of it, cracked open a beer and stared up into the sun. "This is the life."

Garrett and I sat down. He tossed Garrett a beer. He caught it and cracked it open, slugging it back like a man dying of thirst.

"You, champ?" he asked me.

"Sure, why not."

He tossed me a can, I cracked it open, and it spit in my face. When I took my first swallow, it tasted like shit.

I guess he thought this was a big father and son bonding moment. The man was a piece of work.

"So you can see why I had to come out here," he began, as a small group of naked men with long beards and backpacks walked past quite close to us, their private parts wagging.

Garrett and I both looked on in disgust.

"No, not that, idiots," he said and laughed loudly. "But this. The West Coast. Everything about it is larger than life. I didn't know why I headed out here until I got here. Then it sunk in. A new world. New opportunities. Everything just opened up for me."

I was looking up and down the beach and focused on a young, bedraggled couple tucked in behind another drift log. The guy was wrapping something around the girl's arm and had a needle in his hand. I watched in disbelief as he injected something into her arm. It totally freaked me out.

Strangely, Garrett, who had not noticed them, seemed a little more settled than I'd seen him in a long time. "But what about us?" he asked Russell. "Didn't you feel bad about just walking out on Mom and leaving us behind?"

I guess he felt he needed to ask the question again.

Russell lowered his head. "Yes, I did. But your mother and I were having such a hard time. We were arguing so much. Things were just so bad. I felt like I was doing more harm than good by staying. And I had this gut feeling that I was just *supposed* to be somewhere else."

I guess that *somewhere* was here among the big trees, the rich neighbours, the big opportunities, the junkies and the naked old men.

I took another swallow of beer to see if it tasted any better. It didn't.

"You both have a right to judge me. I had plenty of second thoughts. I probably shouldn't tell you this, but not long after I got out here and got my first real estate job, I was in this bar. It was a strip joint, I guess you could say. At a motel on the highway out towards the airport. I had just made my first big sale and I was feeling full of myself. I was on my own, drinking a beer, and this dancer came over to sit with me."

"Jesus, Dad," Garrett said, breaking his rule of calling him that. "Do we really need to hear this?"

"Let me finish," he said. "She came over and sat down. She had a robe on, just for the record. I had no idea why she approached me. But she sat down, and I offered to buy her a drink. She said no. She just said, "I haven't seen you before. What's your story?"

"So I told her my story. She was very patient and listened to every word. She didn't judge. She didn't comment. But then when I finished, she told me, 'Go home. Don't even think about it. They need you. Go home. Just get up right now. Buy a plane ticket and go home to your wife and boys.'

"There was more to it, but she got to me with those words. I left there and was ready to do it. So I went back to my apartment and called your mother. I told her I was coming home. But she told me I wasn't welcome. She told me not to come home. Ever. I asked her to think about it. She hung up on me."

"And that was it?" Garrett asked. "You gave up?"

"I tried calling back. Many times. She wouldn't pick up. But then one day she finally did, and I got an earful again. I took it. Kept saying I was sorry. Told her that, at the very least, I would send money home for her and you boys. She told me no. Said she wouldn't accept a cent."

"And *then* you gave up?"

Russell looked down at the sand he was sitting on and stirred it with a finger. "Yeah, I did. Things were going pretty good here—at least in the business side of my life."

"And the dancer? The stripper?" I asked, almost surprised to hear the words jump out of my mouth.

Garrett looked up at me then. I guess he was thinking the same bizarre thought that had popped into my head.

"I went back there once or twice but she was never there. When I asked about her, they said she'd quit. Moved on to somewhere else."

"Do you remember her name?"

"No. She never said. Never told me. When I asked about her, the other dancers said none of them ever used their real name at the job anyway and no one was going to give it out."

"What did she look like?"

He laughed. "It's funny. I can't remember. She was pretty but that's all. Like I said, I never saw her again."

He finished one beer and then opened another. "So, I guess you could say I closed that chapter on my life and opened another. And I'm sorry. I truly am."

Some more naked people walked by, and I tried not to look. But it was they who looked at us as if we were something odd, something not quite right. And they sure had that correct.

"Chen said you want Garrett to stay here with you," I said. "Is that true?"

168

"Yeah," he answered. "Stay with us, Garrett. Finish high school. GED or whatever. Go to college. UBC maybe or a trade school."

"Chance of a lifetime," Garrett said but I couldn't tell if he was being sarcastic or serious. He couldn't possibly be serious, though.

I decided not to ask about me. It was clear he didn't have any plans for Hopeless. If I'd asked him, he would have probably come up with some bullshit statement about me going home because my mother needed me. Or that I could come out after I was finished high school. But I didn't ask, and he didn't say.

And, besides, I did need to go home. For my mother and for me. And I had no idea what Garrett had up his sleeve. But I had a terrible feeling in the pit of my stomach that whatever happened, I might be losing my brother. Losing him forever.

32

Back at the house, Garrett went into the basement room where we were staying and closed the door. Locked it. The brother who once talked my ear off about everything had turned into a silent, sullen person who shut himself up with his thoughts and didn't let anyone in.

I sat down in the rec room, where Pin was playing a video game—not the violent kind, just some goofy kid thing with cartoon characters and bleeping sounds.

As soon as I sat down, the kid turned off the game and the TV. He must have seen the troubled look on my face, and he said a funny thing. "Homesick?"

"What?"

"Are you homesick? You're a long way from home."

"No. It's not exactly that."

But as soon as I said it, I realized part of me was just that. Homesick. I'd never been away from home ever in my life. Not even a sleepover at a friend's house. Why? Because I never really had any friends. I'd pushed them all away.

Pin was studying me.

"Well, maybe a little. I'm kind of worried about my mom back there all alone. And I kind of miss things."

"Like what?"

"I don't know. Not school. I can live without that. But I miss things that are familiar."

"Me, too," the kid said. "I miss a lot of things."

"Your mother said you lived in Hong Kong."

"Yes. My mom taught at the university there."

"Why'd you leave?"

Pin looked at me with his older-than-six-year-old eyes. "She says she must speak her mind. I think she got in trouble for that."

"Like me. I can never keep my mouth shut. Always getting myself into trouble."

"Things were changing back home. My mom said this wasn't going to be good for us."

"What about your father?"

"He kept telling her everything was going to be okay. But she was sure it wasn't. I think some of my mom's friends even got arrested."

"So you came here."

"Canada has been good to us."

"And my dad?"

"He's okay. He doesn't quite know what to make of me. But he tries."

"More than he did for me."

"I'm sorry to hear that." Again this sounded like the words of someone well beyond his age.

"I wish it wasn't true."

"So now what?" Pin asked. "You gonna stay here with us?"

I shook my head. "I'm not invited. But I can't stay here, anyway. It's not me."

"What about Garrett?"

"Russell wants him to stay."

"Why do you call him Russell?"

"Because he stopped being our father a long time ago," I snapped, maybe directing too much of my resentment Pin's way.

"I get it."

~

The next day, Russell was out of the house early as usual, and Chen drove us to the hospital without us even having to ask.

Walking down those long shiny hallways, I needed to get my brother to talk to me. "Garrett, what is going on with you? You don't talk to me anymore."

"Guess I just don't have much to say."

He was walking at a really fast clip, and he was doing that a lot. As if he didn't want me to keep up, as if he really didn't want me around.

"Can't you just talk to me about whatever's going through your fat head?" I was getting annoyed with the silent treatment and felt I didn't deserve it.

"Can't you just shut up?"

"No, dammit. Talk to me."

He finally stopped dead in his tracks. "What do you want me to say?"

"Tell me you're going to be okay."

"I'm going to be okay," he echoed. "So there."

"Garrett, something is wrong. You need help."

He started walking again. "Oh, fuck off, little brother. You don't know anything about it. And guess what? You won't have to put up with any of my shit anymore. I decided I'm going to stay here. I'm not going back."

"What about Mom?"

"What about her?"

"You're gonna run out on her just like he did."

"It's nothing like that. Look, there's nothing for me back there. I'm here now. I want to see this thing through. I want to be here for Marlene. Jessica said it straight to me. Things are not going well. They both need help."

"But how can you help them?"

"I don't know yet. But I've made up my mind. I'm staying."

"You're going to live with our asshole father?"

"I'll stay for a while. But I'm not staying for *him*. And, you know what? I'm not even sure I'm doing it for Marlene. I'm doing it for me."

"And what about me, asshole?"

"You go home. You go back to being the thorn in the side of every teacher you'll ever have. You go back to being the stubborn nasty little shit you've always been."

We were at Marlene's door now.

"Now shut up and look like you're happy to see her."

He opened the door, and we walked in. Garrett was actually smiling for once, even though it was a big, fake smile.

33

The room was bright today, for a change. Full sunshine. Marlene was sitting up in bed now—well, propped up, I guess you'd say, by the hospital bed that could be adjusted up or down by the push of a button.

Jessica wasn't in the room and Marlene looked more than pleased to see us. Her head was still wrapped in a bandage, but it looked like maybe the bruises on her face were fading a bit. Or it could have just been makeup. But that smile on her face. It wasn't quite right. Was she stoned?

"Welcome to the party," she said.

"What party?" Garrett asked.

Marlene held out her arms. One of them still had the IV line attached. She flapped her arms slowly like a bird. "Well, it was just me and the sunshine until you two showed up." She was definitely high on something.

Garrett looked worried. "You okay?"

"Yes, I actually think so. But it could be the drug they have me on. They won't tell me what it is, but I think it's Oxycontin. I feel like I'm floating."

"Isn't that stuff dangerous?" I asked. "Like addictive or something."

"Honey, I don't think that's much of an issue."

I wanted to ask her what she meant by that, but Garrett's look said, *Shut up.*

"You look good," he said. He was lying, of course, but it must have been the right thing to say.

"C 'mere and give Marlene a hug."

I'd never heard her refer to herself by name before. But then, she was high as a kite.

Garrett bent towards her and let her wrap her arms around him. She held him like that as if she didn't want to let him go, and when she did, Garrett got his arm tangled up in the IV line and nearly ripped it out.

"You, too," she said.

I dutifully leaned into her and felt her arms wrap around me. I closed my eyes for a second and realized something wasn't right. She had very little strength in her arms. And there was a smell. Medicinal, of course. But something else. Not perfume, not body smell. Something different.

When she let go, I was careful not to accidentally pull out the little plastic tube running into her arm.

"How is the West Coast treating you two Bluenosers?" she asked. I hadn't heard that term in a really long time.

"Just great," Garrett said. "I love it here. I've decided to stay."

"What?"

"Yep. Dad offered to put me up and get me into school out here. UBC maybe."

I shot him a nasty look for using the D word.

"No shit?" Marlene said, with a new goofy grin on her face. "That's great. You too?" she asked me.

"Nope," I said. I didn't want to get into it.

"Oh. But you two need to stick together."

"I need to go home to my mom," I said, hoping to curtail the discussion.

"Of course," she said, but I could see a cloud of confusion pass over her face. She turned back to Garrett. "So you and your father are getting along now?"

"We're becoming great pals," he lied, trying to make it sound convincing. "It's like a family reunion. Swapping old stories. Father and son bonding, the whole bit. He even took us to Wreck Beach for some heart-to-heart."

"I'm shocked," she said. "Well, then you did the right thing by coming out here."

I could see something stirring in my brother's mind and didn't know what it was until he opened his mouth again. "Marlene, can I ask you something?"

"Why not? I've got all the time in the world. Ask me anything you want."

Garrett looked like he wasn't quite sure how to ask whatever it was, but he started to piece it together. "Back before you moved east, you were doing that dancing, right?"

"Yes. Jessica and I both were. It was getting us through university."

"You ever work at a bar on the highway to the airport?"

"The Frasier Arms? Yeah, I worked there for maybe four years. Why do you ask?"

"Did you ever run into a guy there from Nova Scotia, someone drinking in the bar, taking in the show—and this guy started talking to you about leaving his wife and coming out here—"

Marlene looked dead serious now but didn't say anything

as Garrett struggled to get the rest of his question out.

"And did you tell him that he should go back home? Go back to his wife and kids?"

I was shocked that Garrett was asking her this. I was even more worried that his curiosity was going to stir up something I didn't want to hear.

Marlene rubbed her hand across her dry lips and then leaned over to pick up a plastic cup with water in it. She took a long drink and then set the cup down as gentle smile came over her face.

"Garrett, do you know how many men told me some sob story back then about leaving home and coming out to Vancouver to start over? Some were single, but some had left wives and families. And they came from Nova Scotia, Newfoundland, New Brunswick, you name it. All the provinces and a few territories. I don't really have a memory of a single one of them, but they all blend together. And I told them all the same damn thing."

I thought she was about to laugh out loud, but the look on Garrett's face must have stopped her.

"Oh," she said. "I get it. You think your father was one of those losers?"

Garrett nodded.

"Well, it could have been me or a dozen other dancers. We probably would have all said the same thing. The whole scene was pretty pathetic, really. Lonely men sitting with their beers, watching us take our clothes off. We only did it for the money—to get us through school or to feed our kids. It wasn't like we were in it for the fun."

I was thinking, *My father the cliché*. Wasn't that just like him? But I still had worse labels for the bastard. And I couldn't believe Garrett was ready to jump ship and take him up on his offer.

Jessica arrived just then. "I see you found some company," she told Marlene. "Flirting with these two again?"

"Telling stories about the good old days," Marlene said. "Do you remember when we were working at the Frasier Arms?"

Jessica sat down in the chair by the bed. "Please, don't remind me. I still have nightmares about it."

Marlene reached out and Jessica took her hand. "Long ago, but it seems like yesterday."

"Well," Jessica said. "Long ago and long gone. That place has been torn down and they built condos there. Good riddance."

"If they could only see me now," Marlene said, lightly tapping the bandage on her head.

"They? They who?" Jessica asked.

"Those men who used to gawk at us at the bar."

"I don't even like to think about them."

"Well, Garrett had just reminded me of them. Funny how some things connect in ways you don't expect."

I didn't exactly understand what she was saying, but Jessica clearly wanted to change the subject.

"Let me get a look at your drip," she said, standing up and looking at the liquid in the bottle that had the tube connected to Marlene's arm. "Just what I thought, you upped the dose a bit on your own, didn't you?"

"Just a tad. They told me I could do it if I felt I needed it."

"More than a tad," Jessica said, sounding like somebody's

mother. "Marlene, you need to be careful."

"Can't a girl have a little fun?"

Jessica leaned over and put a hand on Marlene's forehead. "You're a little warm. You okay?"

Marlene suddenly changed. She was now serious. "No, I'm not okay," she said. "You know that."

"Sorry."

Marlene shut her eyes and almost immediately began to drift off to sleep.

"We should go," Garrett said,

"No," Marlene said. "Let me fall asleep. But stay. I want to know that you're here. I like it when you are here."

"Okay, we'll stay," Garrett said.

So we stayed and watched as she drifted off to whatever dreamland the Oxycontin would bring on.

I leaned on a wall as Garrett hovered by the bed. Jessica put her finger to her lips, and we all stood there in the quiet until Marlene was fast asleep, then she spoke in a hushed tone.

"The doctors did another scan yesterday. The swelling is down from the surgery, but now they're convinced a good part of the tumour is still there. They can't operate again. And radiation or chemo won't do much but...well, prolong things."

She looked out the window and then took a long, deep breath. "I thought you should know."

Garrett looked stunned.

"But what does that mean?" I asked.

Jessica looked like she wished she didn't have to answer the question. "It's just a matter of time. Marlene knows this."

"But she seems so cheerful," I said. "That can't be right."

"Sorry."

She looked like she wanted to say more, but then she just smiled and shooed us out.

I tried to keep up with him as he marched off into the city with me in tow. After about an hour of going nowhere, he just stopped. "We're going back," he said.

34

When we got back, Jessica was adjusting the drip on the IV, which worried me. I wondered if she was supposed to be doing that. I almost reached out to stop her, but I guess she saw me fidget.

"Don't worry. I'm just cutting it back a bit. Marlene is allowed to control how much of the painkiller is going into her, but she gets a little carried away. Not enough to do any real harm. But it's still worrisome."

Garrett looked like he was lost again in his own thoughts. I had gotten used to that in recent months. But it still worried me. He was sitting, but I was pacing around the room.

The noise of me traipsing around must have woken Marlene, because her eyes were wide open now and she was looking around at her audience.

"Can't I get a few smiles in here?" she said. "You all look so bloody serious. This is getting depressing. Lighten up."

But that was hard to do.

"Okay," she said. "Since you're all here, let's have that party."

"C'mon, Mar, be serious," Jessica said.

"Hell, no," was her reply. "I'm tired of serious. Everyone around this damn place is serious. Treating me like some sick kid. I'm tired of it." She was animated, but she was smiling, not frowning. "Let's get this party started."

Garrett was looking at her like she was crazy. Maybe she was. Maybe it was the brain tumour doing this.

But Jessica piped up, "Okay, hon, we'll get some drinks." And then, turning to me, "Nicholas, would you go down to the machines and bring us back some Cokes or something? Anything." She was handing me a twenty-dollar bill.

"Sure," I said.

"And bring me a gin and tonic," Marlene added.

"Coming right up," I said, realizing it was a joke, and more than happy to have a small job to do and take a break from the gloom and now the craziness.

Weird as this may sound, I met a girl at the vending machine. She was having trouble getting it to work and cursing under her breath.

"Let me help," I said.

When she looked at me, she seemed surprised. She had soft dark eyes and long dark hair. "It won't take my money," she said.

I put my twenty into the slot. "What do you want?"

"Just that bottle of water."

I pushed a button and the clear plastic bottle fell down. I reached into the slot and picked it up and handed it to her. We were standing really close together.

"Hey. Thanks. Here, take this." She tried to hand me a five.

"No. It's on me," I said. Mr. Cool, if ever there was one.

She just stood there for a silent second or two.

"You okay?" I foolishly asked.

"Yeah. You?"

I guess we were both thinking that here we were in a hospital, maybe one of us was being treated.

"As good as can be expected," I responded. It was one of my standard comeback lines.

"Hospitals suck."

"They do."

"You're the first person who's been nice to me here," she said.

Nice was never a word that had been used to describe me, I was pretty sure.

"It's nice to be nice sometimes," I said lamely.

This made her laugh. "There's so much pain here. In this place. I don't know how anyone works here."

"Why are you here?"

"My dad."

"Oh, sorry." I didn't have to ask what the problem was. I knew which floor we were on.

"Lots of people are saying that back home. It doesn't help much."

"It never does. Where's back home?"

"Nanaimo. Vancouver Island."

"You live on an island?"

"Yeah. Hey, I gotta get back to my dad. Thanks for this. I owe you one."

"I'll be looking for it. What room?"

"319," she said.

I knew it wouldn't happen. I knew this was a fluke. Girls didn't like me. I usually would try to be funny and say something stupid. I'd never had a girlfriend. Not one. Not even close to having one.

Now, here I was in Vancouver General Hospital, and had met this girl I wanted to get to know. Hell, I wanted more than that.

But what a weird experience. I was convinced that I'd go all the way through high school and never have a girlfriend, never even have a girl who liked me. And now this.

What was I thinking? It was all just in my head.

As I stared at my reflection in the shiny glass of the vending machine, though, I saw someone different there. Despite all the gloom and doom around here, this sucker had a quirky smile on his mug. Jesus.

My money was still in the machine. I punched some codes that sent down four cans of something. I don't even remember what.

~

When I opened the door to the room, I could tell the three of them were in the midst of an intense conversation, but they seemed to immediately clam up.

"And here's the man of the hour," Jessica said. "Let the party begin."

"Sorry," I told Marlene. "They were all out of gin and tonic."

"Just my luck," she said. She was sitting perfectly upright now, and her eyes were clear, not cloudy like before. I handed her a can.

"Perfect," she said. "Zero sugar. I do need to watch my weight."

Then she took a good look at me. "What is that look,

Nicky? What is that look on your face?"

"Nothing."

"Not nothing, kid. Must be something."

I may have blushed just then. "Oh, I was talking to this girl at the vending machine."

They all burst out laughing, although Marlene put her hand over her mouth to subdue herself.

"Romeo on the roam," Jessica said.

"Nothing like that."

"Well, was she cute?"

"Yes."

"Did you get her number?"

"Well, sort of," I said, thinking that, yes, I knew in which room she was visiting her sick father. But they laughed some more.

At least I thought they were all laughing, but when I turned to Garrett, I saw that he wasn't. He looked like he wasn't there at all. He was someplace else.

"Maybe the West Coast agrees with you," Jessica said. "Maybe you should stay on out here as well."

But that was never going to happen. I missed home. I missed my mom and even my old bedroom. Whatever happened next, I knew I was losing Garrett. And I didn't know how I was going to deal with that. But I'd been losing him for many months already.

Jessica was telling Garrett to lighten up and join the so-called party. But there was some secret signal in the way she said it to him.

The little party wound down pretty quickly. Marlene began to fade and, before long, Jessica announced, "Party's over. The princess needs her beauty sleep."

Jessica ushered the two of us out the door, shushing us as we went. Once we were out of the room, she put her arm around Garrett and hung back from me as we walked down the hall.

I wasn't supposed to hear what she was whispering in his ear. But I caught some of it anyway.

"Just think about it," she said.

35

Garrett was acting weirder than ever as we left the hospital.

"I don't want to go back to Russell's house," he said. "I just want to walk. Can you find your way back?"

"I don't want to go back there either," I said.

"Then let's go downtown and see what this friggin' city is like."

"Yeah," I echoed. "Let's check out this friggin' city."

Garrett closed his eyes and seemed to be sniffing the air. Without further discussion, he started off in a different direction from Point Grey.

I didn't ask any questions. It was a fine day, and he was lost in thought as was so often the case with him. But this time there was something different.

We eventually arrived at a little bay, and I saw a sign that said False Creek. Garrett had sniffed out saltwater and followed it.

Across the water we could see the gleaming towers of downtown. It didn't look like Halifax at all. More like something from a science fiction movie.

When we got to Cambie Street we found a bridge to cross over.

Garrett stopped in the middle of the bridge and looked

down. The water looked dirty, and it wasn't flowing. I guessed that was what the False Creek bit was. Just a dead-end arm of water. Like the Northwest Arm back in Halifax. Only different.

Everything was different here, but it made me think back to what seemed like the carefree days of our childhood. Swimming in the Arm in the summer. Frigging around on the ice in the winter. And wasn't that how we met Marlene, in what seemed like a lifetime ago?

"What were you guys talking about when I came back?"

"We were talking about how ugly you were," he said, joking, suddenly sounding more like my old older brother who would tease me relentlessly. But the same older brother who was always looking out for me.

"Yeah. And what conclusion did you come to?"

"That you're definitely ugly. But not the ugliest kid on the planet."

"Oh. That's comforting."

And it was. Garrett and I used to bullshit like this. It was a verbal game. A stupid game for sure. But endearing. *You're so stupid that…You're so gullible that…You're so ugly that…*And then we'd maybe hit each other with pillows and laugh our asses off. But no one was laughing now.

"No, really."

"You really want to know?"

"Yeah."

A couple of motorboats were going under the bridge now. Two young guys in ball caps looked up and waved to us. And then they were gone.

Then he told me what Jessica had said, plus some stuff

about an experimental drug that would maybe extend Marlene's life for a while. But it wouldn't cure her.

It sounded more desperate than what Jessica or Marlene had let on to me.

"That's what you talked about?"

"There's more. I don't know if you want to hear it."

"I want to hear it."

"Marlene said no to the radiation. And she wants to say no to the chemo. She says she's been through enough."

"But they can't just let her die."

"That's not quite it."

"What, then?"

"She doesn't want to spend the rest of her days in that hospital bed. She asked the doctors for a different way to end her life."

Garrett was looking down at the water of False Creek now in the direction of the salty wind. The sea was out there somewhere. He took a deep breath, let it out again.

"Assisted suicide? That's crazy."

"Not so crazy, really," Garrett said. "And suicide is not the right word, The technical term is Medical Assistance in Dying, or MAID. It would be hard for you to understand. But I think I get it."

"When?"

"That's the problem. There is no when. They turned her down."

"So it won't happen? So she'll have to take the treatment?"

Garrett said nothing at first. It was as if he was focused on something in the far distance. Something I couldn't see.

"It won't happen, right?" I repeated.

"The doctors won't do it. Can't do it. They have committees that decide these things. The committee said no, so none of them can do it. They'd lose their license. Or worse."

"So maybe they're wrong about the diagnosis. Maybe that new drug will kick in and work."

"Even if it works, they say it might only help, not cure. They call it a plateau. Even if it works, it just means she won't get any worse—for a while. They refer to it as extending life. That's all. *Extending*. Like she said, we're all going to die."

"Fuck that bullshit," I said. I knew we were all going to die. But we all wanted to live first. We wanted to stay alive.

"That's right, little brother. Fuck that bullshit. That's what I've been feeling about a lot of things. But I understand what she's feeling. And thinking. I really do. I mean, she's so different from us, but ever since we met her, she's been the one who got me through every bad thing that has happened to me."

"What bad things? Sure, our lame father ran out on us back when we were kids, but we did okay. You had your shit together more than me. What bad things?"

Garrett shook his head. He picked up a rock from the side of the road and dropped it into the brownish water below. "The bad things going through my head. I could never really explain it to you or Mom. But it was bad. It still is bad, sometimes."

I understood that this had something to do with the moodiness, the dark phases my brother went through as we got older. But, like Mom had said, I too thought it was a

190

phase of life he'd grow out of. "That doesn't make sense."

He turned and looked at me now. "Not to you, you little shit. You had it in you, too. But you let it out. Aside from Mom and me, you were a royal pain in the ass to everyone you met. Why was that? Tell me."

I didn't have an answer for him. Because I didn't know. It had just been my way of coping with the same set of circumstances Garrett and I shared. I guess I knew I had some control of something if I had the power to piss off whoever I wanted to piss off.

Garrett picked up a larger stone and threw it into the water. We both watched as it hit and make those circles that moved out across the water. "Jessica can't bring herself to do it," he said, changing the subject abruptly.

"Can't do what?"

"What Marlene wants."

I now knew what Marlene wanted. And I suddenly had a vision of horrible things. Stuff I'd seen on TV shows.

"It's pretty simple, really," Garrett continued. "The machine with the drip. It's automated. Marlene can control some of it herself—the Oxy—and so can Jessica if she sees the need. But it's monitored and it's limited. But there's a code for the machine. It can be adjusted more by someone who knows the code."

"Like for an overdose?"

"Yes."

"But Jessica refuses to do it?"

"They've loved each other for quite a while. They still love each other."

"Why does she want to die?"

"She's in pain. She doesn't want to suffer. She doesn't want to be a burden. She doesn't want to live out the rest of her life in a hospital bed in a drug-induced daze. It makes sense."

"Okay, I see that. But how the hell did she get the code? I can't imagine the hospital gave it to her so she could commit suicide! Jesus! This is unbelievable. And if she's got the code, why doesn't she use it?"

"Keep your voice down! One of the nurses—she wouldn't say which one. She gave her some strong hints about the code's numbers so she wouldn't be implicated directly. But as much as Marlene wants to go peacefully, and when she chooses, she just can't do it."

I was having a hard time keeping my patience. "So she's out of options. End of discussion."

"There is an option," he said, not looking at me. "Marlene asked me to do it."

I guess I should have seen that coming but I didn't. "And you said no, right?"

"I didn't say anything."

"Don't do it."

"Marlene has never asked us to do one thing for her. The whole time we knew her back home. Not once. And she was always there for us, right? Always there to listen and to make things seem better than they were."

"You can't do it."

"Why not?"

"Because the hospital—that committee or whoever—will find out. And they'll hold you accountable."

"Maybe."

"There will be an investigation. The Oxycontin. They'll know. And it will go badly."

"Maybe."

"But you'll be looked at as a murderer. You'll be tried as an adult."

"Probably."

"That's why you can't do it."

Garrett just stood there staring off into space, thinking something, I didn't know what, but I could tell he had his mind made up.

"Let me do it," I finally said. "Tell Jessica. Tell Marlene. If I get blamed, it will be different because of my age. We'll find the code somehow and, if Marlene really wants it, I'll do it."

36

"That's not going to happen," Garrett said flatly. "Don't be stupid. Marlene wouldn't let you. I won't let you. Just get it out of your head."

But I couldn't get it out of my head. I didn't want to think about Marlene dying, but ever since we got out here and saw the shape she was in at the hospital, everything seemed different. The rules were different. Maybe there really is a point when you want to die and it's the right thing to do.

"Wanna keep walking or go back to Russell's?" Garrett asked, obviously feeling he had made his point. End of conversation.

"You?"

"I wanna walk."

"Then let's walk."

As we finished crossing the bridge, Garrett led us to a rundown part of town. There were quite a few scruffy-looking people on the street, some begging for change, some asleep in sleeping bags on the sidewalk. One guy approached us and asked Garrett if he "needed anything." Garrett said no.

A couple of women were fighting on the sidewalk. I'd never seen women fighting before. It was ugly and frightening and made me think I'd lived a rather sheltered life.

We just kept on walking. Garrett turned one way and then another and my feet were hurting but I didn't say a word. He'd stop now and then and sniff the air. Like a dog, I was thinking.

But I quickly figured out he was trying to smell the sea. We were in the midst of tall glass buildings at that point and all I could smell was city smells—food cooking, car exhaust, the stench of garbage.

Eventually we came to some water and the entrance to a park of some sort with giant trees. Stanley Park, the sign said. There were paths along the water and that's where we headed.

I couldn't believe the trees.

We must have looped around a peninsula, because we eventually found our way back to where we'd entered this amazing place.

"I'm tired," Garrett finally said. "Let's go get some rest."

As we returned to the noisy city, he suddenly started waving his arms at the traffic. A cab driver saw us and stopped.

"West Point Grey," he told the driver, who was wearing a turban.

"You got money?" the man asked.

Garrett reached in his pocket and showed him a handful of bills.

"Get in."

We got in.

I was wondering where Garrett got the money, but I didn't have to ask. No doubt it came from dear old Dad trying to buy his way back into our lives. "Guilt money," they call it.

No one said a word on the drive after that. Not the driver. Not Garrett. Not me.

That night Chen cooked a dinner for us. She seemed quite proud of it. There was small talk and Russell was quite cheerful or at least faking cheerful. Pin sat quietly and ate.

Garrett was back to his moody self and left the table before the meal was over. We each had a room in Russell's big-ass house, and when I checked his room later, it was empty.

Pin asked if I wanted to watch some movie with him involving Godzilla fighting some other monster. I forget which one. I told him not tonight, and he seemed disappointed.

It was still light out and my head was buzzing. I had to get out of there. I decided I had to get back to Marlene on my own.

The thing I needed to do needed to be done right away if it was going to be done at all. No more discussion with Garrett. No more thinking about it.

Russell hung back in the kitchen, drinking a glass of wine with Chen. I'd seen him set his wallet on the desk in the room he called his home office. I slipped in there and relieved him of some more guilt money without him offering.

Pin had been dogging me, asking if I'd play a board game or hang out with him. He saw me take the money. I put my finger to my lips, and he nodded but he looked quite unhappy about what I was doing.

And then I was out the door, without anyone else noticing. It was a warm evening and it felt good—it felt right—to be on my own.

I hoofed it through Kitsilano and across the Burrard Street Bridge and saw more of those taxis lined up outside a hotel. I got in the first one in line. A young-looking driver had some earbuds in and didn't even notice me at first.

"Hospital please," I said, tapping on his shoulder.

He popped out the earbuds. "Like an emergency?"

"No. Visiting an old friend. Vancouver General. You know where it is?"

He gave me a dirty look. I guessed that was the wrong thing to ask.

~

When I entered the front door of the hospital, a woman in a nurse's uniform informed me it was after visiting hours and I'd have to come back the next day. I said I would but just wanted to use the washroom first and she said okay.

In the washroom, I looked at myself in the mirror. Was I really here to do this deed? Was it really the right thing to do? The boy in the mirror said to get the hell out of there. Forget about it.

But all my life I'd taken everything like a joke. I'd treated all my teachers poorly, never really had any friends who would put up with my negativity. Even Garrett had given up on me, it had seemed.

Until now.

I splashed some cold water onto my face and then looked deep into my own eyes. I was never one to study myself in the mirror. I had to admit that I barely knew the face I was looking at. Was it that of a boy or a man? Clearly, it was a boy. And that's why I was the one to do the job.

I rubbed the water off with a paper towel, quickly left the washroom and found the stairwell that would take me up to the cancer ward. I ran up the stairs and no one saw me. But I had to stop and catch my breath before opening the door onto the hallway.

As I breathed heavily, trying to get a grip on myself, I still wasn't sure I could do this thing. If I was caught, would they call me a murderer? I tried not to think about it. If I didn't do it, and Garrett did, then it would be him who would get the label. Somehow that bothered me even more.

I stopped thinking about it, took another deep breath, opened the stairway door and saw an empty hallway. I made a run for Marlene's room and slipped inside without being seen.

Jessica was still there, stretched out on a reclining chair that doubled as a bed. She was asleep, but Marlene was lying on her back, her eyes wide open. I startled her as I approached the bed.

But then she reached for the remote near her hand and raised the bed up so that she was in a sitting position. She leaned to her left and looked at the IV drip and pushed a small button that made the monitor beep.

"Where's Garrett?" she whispered.

"I came alone."

"Oh. Okay. Well, that's nice of you. But isn't it after visiting hours?"

"It is. I let myself in. I don't tend to follow rules very well." I was just about getting ready to explain why I was here, but she wanted to talk.

"I remember. Anyway, I'm glad you're here. I was thinking about your question. About your father. Maybe it *was* him. He was a young man. And handsome. But I wasn't interested in that. Jessica and I were hoping to save enough money to buy a little cabin out on one of the Gulf Islands. Somewhere on the water. Away from it all. We thought that if we could just get there and put all this behind us, life would be...well, wonderful."

"But what about him?" I interrupted. "The man who had left his family."

"After you mentioned it, I remembered. He was from Nova Scotia. He said he had two kids. Two boys. He bragged about the older one. He told me a name, but I forget what he said. I kept thinking if he was so proud of this kid, why did he just get up and leave? Then I asked him about the younger boy. And he shook his head. I remember what he said now. He said, 'Oh, that one. That one is nothing but a pain in the ass. That one is hopeless.' That's how big a shit your father was. Or maybe I'm mixing him up with one of those dozens of others. Or maybe it's these drugs messing up my mind. I probably shouldn't have told you. But there it is."

"What else did he say?"

"I don't know. He seemed to want me to feel sorry for him. The poor slob."

"And did you?"

She looked a little embarrassed. "I pretended to. I was good at that. It was an act. So when he was finished with his sob story, he gave me some money. A tip."

"And?"

"And I never saw him again. Whoever that run-of-the-mill jerk was. Jessica and I soon finished our university degrees. We had saved enough money to get the hell out of there. Land on the islands was still fairly cheap. We bought a little two-room cabin from an old codger. Right on the shore. Facing east, where we could watch the sun come up over the water."

Then she took a quick deep breath. I detected a twinge of pain on her face as she moved her head from side to side as if to try to shake it off. "But, you know, now that I think about it, it's really pretty unlikely that was actually your father."

I didn't say anything, since I had more important things on my mind, but I was convinced it had been him.

"Garrett told me what you wanted him to do," I suddenly blurted out.

"I told him not to tell anyone."

"He told me."

"He shouldn't have."

"He did."

"Is that why you're here?"

"Yeah. I needed to talk to you."

"Okay. Talk," she said.

"I can't let Garrett do what you asked him," I said.

"I understand."

"Why are you so sure this is what you want?"

She looked up at the ceiling now. "I wasn't at first. I was sure I wanted everything they could give me. But I've been over this with nearly a dozen doctors. They've got brain scans. They can show me what's going on. The surgery nearly killed me. The pain was horrible. And so was the memory loss. I didn't know who I was or where I was. That will come again as things get worse. They can't do a second operation. They're pretty sure more radiation will be too much, as well. And it wouldn't be enough to stop the tumour anyway."

"But the chemo, that could help. Right?"

"Could."

"Why not do it?"

She threw her hands up in the air slightly, but the motion seemed to trigger more pain. I could see it in her eyes. "I already am. And it may be slowing things down some, but that's all. But look at me."

I'd tried not to focus on how pale she looked, how frail, how completely unlike the lively, energetic woman Garrett and I had met the day we almost got swept out to sea. "I don't really expect you to understand."

"So you made this decision, and the doctors turned you down?"

"I was sure they'd understand. Assisted suicide is not common. But somewhat accepted in my circumstance. But there have been legal issues here at this hospital. Apparently, the timing of my request was not good."

"But there is a plan?"

"Yes. I know the code for the machine."

I nodded toward Jessica. "Why doesn't she do this for you?"

That soft sorrowful smile came over her weary face. "We've discussed it many times. We've known each other a long time. We love each other." It looked like she wanted to say more but she had to stop and take a drink of water.

Jessica turned on her side and I was hoping she would not wake up. Not just yet.

"Why don't you do it yourself, then? I saw you adjust something there. Why get anyone else involved?"

Marlene said nothing, but Jessica had heard me. She sat up and it took her a few seconds to figure out what was going on.

"She can't bring herself to do it," she said. "We've talked about it a lot. She just can't."

Marlene put a hand to her forehead and then held it out to me. I took her hand and held it. "I have thought long and hard about this. Maybe it's my religious upbringing or maybe it's because I'm weak. Or scared. Or all three. I just can't. I'm sorry. I wish I could."

"But you asked Garrett?"

"I didn't, really. He heard Jessica and me talking. He volunteered."

Just like him. Trying to be the hero. But this was different. "But now I'm volunteering." I tried to explain my logic. "Besides, no one will know."

"I'll know," Jessica said.

"But you won't tell."

"No. But the staff here. They'll figure it out."

"And if they do, tell them it was me."

"You'd do this for me?" Marlene asked. "Take the risk?"

My thoughts were firing like bullets in my head. I was in very deep. But right then I wasn't scared at all. "What is it you want most?" I asked Marlene.

"I want the pain to go away."

"Okay," I said. I looked at the IV bag. It was nearly full. I looked at the machine that controlled the drip.

"Just tell me the code," I said.

Marlene didn't answer, so I looked over to Jessica. She was wringing her hands and looking straight at me.

37

"Not yet," Marlene said. "Get up here."

I didn't understand what she meant at first.

"Up here on the bed. Lie beside me."

It wasn't what I was expecting. I looked at Jessica and she just nodded.

So I gingerly crawled up alongside of Marlene to lie down beside her. I just lay there at first, listening to her ragged breath, but then I felt her arm curl around me.

"Close your eyes," she said.

With my eyes closed, I felt myself swirling into a pool of darkness. I tried to focus on what I had decided. What I was about to do. I ignored the inner voice that was screaming to me, *Don't do it. Just get up and leave. Never come back.*

Marlene began to hum a song I didn't recognize, but it faded quickly as she began to have trouble breathing.

When she stopped, she took a couple of deep breaths to recover, and I felt her hand touch my forehead. "I wish you were my son," she said.

It came out of the blue and shocked the hell out of me. I said nothing.

We lay like that for what seemed like a long time. I couldn't speak because I was feeling something deep within me that I can't quite describe. It was like my whole understanding of the world had been off. I'd been wrong about so much. Angry and resentful of everyone. Uncertain and untrusting of just about everything. And this, her strange words just confused me more.

But now something changed. I realized that I'd come into the room full of bluster, ready to do something that I had not really thought deeply about. Now I understood what I *had* to do, what I'd volunteered to do. And Marlene had just given me the courage to do it. I could truly accept whatever came after.

I could do this thing. I could stop the pain.

I opened my eyes. I was lying there looking at the ceiling. All I had to do was stand up, walk to the other side of the bed. And do what Marlene wanted so much.

But then that's when I heard it. The beeping. Someone was punching in the code.

I sat bolt upright and there was Jessica. She was looking at the machine and then up at the IV bag. "It's done," she said. "Nicholas, stay right there. Don't move."

I was frozen. I couldn't move even though I suddenly wanted to get up out of there and run. But I didn't.

And suddenly Marlene pulled herself upright in the bed and stared at Jessica. "No!" she shouted, and then she ripped the IV tube out of her arm.

I pulled myself away from Marlene, up and out of the bed. I saw some blood coming from Marlene's arm where she had ripped the tube out.

As I moved away, Jessica leaned over and put her arms around Marlene. The two women were embracing and crying softly as the machine began to beep loudly.

I clumsily made my way around the bed and ripped the plug of the beeping machine out of the wall. But even as I did so, another alarm of some sort went off in the room.

"You should leave now," Jessica said. "Go. Quickly. Just go."

I heard footsteps in the hall almost immediately and the door opened. A nurse and a young doctor burst into the room. Jessica looked straight at me and silently mouthed the word again. *Go.*

38

And then everything changed.

And nothing changed.

Decisions had been made. Decisions had been reversed.

Marlene was still sick. She was still in pain. She was still dying. I had tried to help. At least I thought I was helping. But now I was more confused than ever over what had just happened.

I raced down the stairs and out the front door of the hospital.

I don't remember much of the long walk back to Point Grey. I remember standing by the seawall in Kitsilano with the moon shining on the water. I remember thinking that I had, for once in my life, mustered up some courage to do a very difficult thing—what I thought was the right thing—and then it was taken away. I was happy Marlene was still alive, but what else?

So much more. What she'd said to me in the bed. That didn't make any sense. But not much did. Not much ever did. So much confusion.

Maybe I was feeling what Garrett felt like. Nothing was right. Nothing made sense. Maybe it never would. Maybe there was no place for me in the world.

The water looked inviting. I kept walking along the seawall until I came to the place that had rental canoes. I wanted to get in one and just drift out into the bay, sit there with the moon shining down for a while. Or just get in it and drift away.

There was enough light from the moon that I could poke around looking for one that wasn't chained up properly. The chains were old and rusty, and I eventually found one I could snap when I yanked it hard enough. Under another canoe was a broken paddle.

So I did it. I dragged the one-man canoe across the sand and slid it into the calm water. I got my feet wet walking it out into the shallows and then I got in.

I took ten long strokes and then I tilted my head back and just looked up at the sky. I drifted far from shore and soon felt the tug of a current under me. The canoe rocked gently side to side and felt unstable, so I moved off the seat and sat down on the floor, tucked my feet into the front of the canoe and leaned back on the seat, looking up at the sky, still bright with moonlight and not a single star.

The current had me in its grip and, when I looked back, I could see the bright lights of the city and realized that wherever I was going, I was drifting away, probably out to sea. Was that what I really wanted? Maybe.

But something else.

In my mind, it was winter again back in Nova Scotia. And I was drifting with the ice out into the Atlantic. I was scared. And I didn't want to end this way.

The realization of my predicament paralyzed me again—almost the same way I had felt frozen there in Marlene's bed.

And then something came up alongside. Something dark from the depths. It surfaced and then dove, surfaced and then dove. Whatever it was, it seemed to be staying with me. And no, it wasn't anything that I was afraid of. I didn't feel threatened. I didn't exactly feel safe, but at least I didn't feel like I was alone.

I focused on some scattered lights to my left now and understood that there was the shoreline. But those lights stopped not far down the coast. That would have meant where the peninsula ended. Beyond that, the Georgia Straight. Then the open sea.

I picked up the paddle and got back up on the seat. Frantically, I stroked with the broken paddle, trying to angle the canoe towards those final lights along the shore.

The sea creature stayed with me. A seal most likely. Or a dolphin. Maybe even a young orca. I'll never know.

It took a long while. I was not much of a paddler. I talked to the creature. I talked to myself. I kept my eyes on the flickering lights ashore until I heard small waves lapping, a sound I will never forget.

At that point, I decided to put my hand into the water to see if I could touch whatever companion this was who had stayed with me. But he was gone.

Maybe he'd never been there.

But it didn't matter. I was ashore. Cold and wet but ashore.

As I pulled the canoe up out of the water onto the gravelly beach, an old man came out of the darkness to help me. In the moonlight I could see he had long hair and an even longer beard.

"Shouldn't be out in the water at night, son," he said. "You all right?"

"I think so," I said. "Where am I?"

"Wreck Beach."

"How did you see me?"

"I live here," he said. "I see everything."

"Everything?"

"Everything." He paused and then said, "You want me to make you some tea?" It was the oddest thing to hear.

"No thanks."

"What do you need? I can help."

"I need to get home," I said. And it was what I really meant. I needed to get home to Nova Scotia. But this old homeless guy living at Wreck Beach wasn't going to be able to do that.

"Well, I can at least guide you up the trail."

"Please."

The trail up from the beach was very steep. And I would never have found my way if he had not been my guide. I had to stop at least ten times from being winded, although he seemed to be just fine.

At the top we arrived at a parking lot with streetlights overhead. I recognized the university buildings across the street.

"Gonna be okay?" he asked.

"Maybe," I said.

"Maybe is good," he said, and with that he turned and disappeared back onto the forest trail.

I knew where I was, and I knew that I just had to follow

the coastal road at the top of the cliffs here and it would take me back to West Point Grey and my father's house. It wasn't home but it would have to do.

I was cold and exhausted.

39

My exhaustion took me into a deep sleep, and I didn't wake easily in the morning.

Pin knocked on my door near noon and asked if I would go for a walk down to the beach with him to look at seabirds.

"Where's Garrett?" I asked.

"Gone to visit that friend of yours a long time ago."

"Damn," I said angrily. "Why didn't he wake me?"

"I don't know." Pin looked hurt. He was always trying to be my friend and I was always pushing him away.

"Sorry, Pin. I need to get to the hospital."

He looked disappointed as he backed out of my room, and I suddenly felt sorry for him. He was a lonely little kid —the little brother I never had, maybe. But that was *my* role. I had always been the little brother up until the time Garrett shut me out.

Chen and Russell were both gone. How odd that they'd leave him alone with only me as the other person in the house. I looked around for some cash again. Easy enough to find in a drawer in the kitchen. I don't know what Pin must have been thinking as he saw me take the money again.

As he was looking at me with a pained expression, I

asked him, "How do I get a cab?"

He just took his phone out of his pocket, made the call and gave the address. "Can I come with you?" he asked.

"Sorry. But no." Pin looked disappointed. And then I said, "Oh, shit. I can't leave you alone in the house."

"I'll be okay."

"Not good enough," I said. "Any place nearby you can hang out? Some place with an adult?"

Pin didn't seem to want to answer.

"C'mon, I'm in a hurry."

"My friend Jacob lives three doors down. His mom works from home. She's always there."

And she was. I walked Pin over there and tried to explain the situation to Jacob's mother who, in the end, ushered him inside. Then I took off.

I had no idea what I would find at the hospital. Maybe the drama was over. Or maybe Garrett had decided to take things into his own hands. I just didn't understand much of what went through his head these days.

I began to realize that he never intended to let me be the one to do the deed. What was the term? Mercy killing?

My head was swimming with thoughts of the night before. The hospital, the bay. The old guy on the beach and the long, cold walk home.

~

When I got to the hospital, I ran inside and took the stairs instead of waiting at the elevator, where there was a crowd. I passed several young, smiling hospital workers on the stairway. They were chatting and laughing, and it just seemed all wrong for them to be doing that in a building filled with sick and dying patients. I wanted to tell them to fuck off, but I had more important things on my mind.

A hefty young man in a security uniform spotted me as I was passing the nursing station. I was running at that point, and he put out his arms to block me.

"Whoa. Whoa," he said. "What's the hurry?"

I was out of breath and really didn't have an answer for him. "Just let me by, please."

"Where are you going?"

I couldn't remember the room number. But I pointed to the door down the hall. "Marlene," I said. "Her name is Marlene."

The security guard looked back at the nurse on duty at the desk and she shook her head no.

"Can't let you down there."

"Why not?"

"Just can't. Come with me."

He had a hand on my shoulder now. This felt all wrong. But he was way stronger than me. I didn't know where he was leading me, but it was the wrong direction.

I let him guide me at first, as other people in the hall looked on. But it was the look on the face of the young nurse at the desk that got to me. Something was not right.

I just waited for the pressure of his hand on my shoulder to lighten up, and then I twisted myself around and bolted for Marlene's room. He was right behind me but not fast enough to catch me before I burst through the door.

Garrett was sitting by the window, staring out. Jessica

was sitting in the chair where she always sat, but she had her head down and her hands together. Was she praying?

Marlene was not in the bed.

Before I could say anything, the guard grabbed me from behind and pinned me against the wall. Garrett was immediately on his feet and ready to pounce on the security guard, but Jessica stood up.

"Wait!" she shouted. "Back off."

He backed off.

"It's okay," she said. "He's family."

That seemed to do the trick. The guy took a step back. He put his hands up. "We got rules, you know?"

"I know," she said. "I'm sorry for your trouble."

And he was good with that. He backed out the door and let it shut behind him.

"Where's Marlene?" I asked, expecting the worst. "Where is she?"

There was a strange pause as Jessica took a deep breath. "She's in surgery," she began, but she could tell from the look on my face that she needed to explain more. "It's nothing major. She's getting an implant—a port it's called—for the IV. So she doesn't have to have a needle jammed into her arm. We both decided it was the thing to do."

I didn't fully understand.

"But she's not getting more surgery for the tumour?" I asked.

"No. The doctors say it would be too dangerous. Not worth the risk."

"Then what?"

"We have a plan," Jessica said. "We talked about it. The

three of us."

"What kind of plan?" I still didn't like the sound of it. And why the three of them?

"Marlene doesn't want to stay here. And I didn't think I could handle everything that needs to be done on my own."

Garrett walked towards me now and looked me in the eye. "So I said I would stay on and help."

"Help?"

"We're going to take her to the island," Jessica said. "To Gabriola. She'll be on a treatment that will stabilize her for a while. We'll have the pain meds. Once the port is in, we'll be able to handle it. Garrett and me. I can do this if he's there to help."

Garrett nodded. He had lost that lost-soul look, that injured-dog look. Something in him had changed. "I *want* to do this," he said. "You didn't think I was going to stay on in that suburban nightmare with our asshole father, did you?"

"But it's an island," I said. "Is there a hospital there?"

"There's a clinic," Jessica said, "but no, not a real hospital."

"Is that wise?" I asked.

"It's what Marlene wants," Garrett told me. "To wake up and see the sunrise over the water. To be where she wants to be instead of cooped up in here."

"But when the time comes…" I began, but I couldn't finish the sentence.

"When the time comes, she'll be where she wants to be," Jessica said.

"And we'll be there," Garrett added.

"Like family?"

"Yes," Jessica said. "Like family."

Maybe on some level this really did make sense. If you were going to die, didn't you want to do it on your own terms? And not in a hospital but someplace you really cared about?

I walked over to the window and sat down, confused by what was going through my head. It was the weirdest thing. I was feeling hurt. I was feeling sorry for myself. I was not going to be part of this family.

I know Garrett understood exactly what I was thinking. "You have to go home to Mom. You have to try to explain it to her. And you have to be there for her. She was always good to us."

Right then, I didn't want to go home. Back to my old life, but without Garrett. And what else? Go back to school? Back to all that same old shit.

"Maybe you and Mom can some visit us. On the island."

I knew that would never happen. And I knew I'd never see Marlene again after I flew home. Would I ever see Garrett again?

After a long period of silence, with me just looking out the window, Jessica began to describe the cottage and the island. It sounded a bit primitive, but she made it sound wonderful. I hoped that someday I really would get to see it.

But the more she described it, the more convinced I was that, in the not-so-distant future, Marlene would be gone. And Garrett would be out of my life as well. He'd been gone in a way for quite a while, but now he would be a continent away.

I didn't want to say what I was really feeling. Decisions

had been made. And it was probably the best for everyone. Everyone but me.

"Anyone want something to drink?" I asked, checking to see how much money I had in my pocket.

Nobody did. "I'll be right back," I said. I just needed to get out of there. There was so much to sink in.

I half expected to see the girl at the vending machine. But there was just me. The guard eyed me suspiciously from behind the desk. But he didn't say anything. I put in some money and punched the button for a bottle of water.

When I returned to the room, two staff workers were lifting Marlene into her bed. Once she was settled and they had left, she motioned for me to come to her.

I leaned over and noticed the large bandage on her chest. The port.

Her eyes seemed to have a hard time focusing, but a smile slowly crept across her face. "Now they don't have to jab me in the arm anymore. Ever see such a thing?"

She held out her hand and I took it. It felt very warm, and she had a weak grip. "Did they explain the plan?" she asked.

I nodded. "Can't I come along for the ride?"

"Nope. You gotta get back home and make a life for yourself."

"So I've been told."

"You read all those books I left you?"

"Some?"

"Finish *Karamazov* yet?"

"No."

"Read the ending."

"Without reading the whole thing?"

218

"Sure. Why not?"

I realized now she was sounding a little stoned, but it was probably whatever they gave her for the operation.

"What about Kerouac?"

At first, I didn't know what she was referring to.

"*On the Road*," Garrett said. "I left it at Russell's house. Take it with you."

"Read the end of that one, too," Marlene said, as if the whole thing was a game.

"Do I have to write a book report?" I asked.

"Something like that. Read all the others when you get a chance."

I thought about that dusty pile of books back in our house—all the ones she had left us when she moved out here. Really, is that what she wanted to say most to me? Read the damn books?

"Then write one of your own someday, okay?"

That was a joke. Me, a writer? No way.

"Sure," I said. "I'll dedicate it to you."

"I'd like that," she said. "Oh my, but I'm so tired."

Jessica got up and quickly moved to her side. "You need something? You want me to call the nurse?"

Marlene waved her hand in the air. "No, no, no. I'm just tired. Nicholas, you need to start working on your storytelling. Tell me a story. Anything at all."

It was an odd request. I looked at Jessica, who just shrugged. When I looked at Garrett, he nodded.

So I told her the story about Garrett and me and the drifting ice on the Northwest Arm back in Nova Scotia, what seemed so very long ago. When I got to the part of the two of us in frozen wet clothes, I realized she was fast asleep.

On my way out that afternoon, I met the girl from the vending machine. "How's your dad?" I asked.

"Better," she said. "Much better." She was smiling and seemed happy to see me. "And your friend?"

"She's amazing," I said.

And we stood there like that for a few more awkward seconds. We really didn't have more to say to each other, but there was something uplifting about making this connection to this girl whose name I didn't even know. Something that told me that girls—people—might see me as a kindred spirit, not just a pissed-off kid.

Something that told me I had changed.

40

I stayed one more week in Vancouver, hanging around, waiting until the hospital would release Marlene. Garrett and I walked through as many parts of the city as we could get to on foot. Most days, we'd end up at Stanley Park and hike through the giant trees. Then we'd go visit Marlene. She seemed better—stronger at least. But not cured, of course.

Russell argued with Garrett about his new plan, his new life. But in the end, he gave up trying to convince his son to stay.

The day before I flew home, Garrett joined Marlene and Jessica in a special-care vehicle that would drive them to the docks and then onto the ferries that would take them to Gabriola Island.

Garrett left me a few things to take home to Nova Scotia, including a handwritten letter to Mom and his dog-eared copy of *On the Road*. I read the last paragraph:

> So in America when the sun goes down and I sit on the old broken-down river pier watching the long, long skies over New Jersey and sense all that raw land that rolls in one unbelievable huge bulge over to the West Coast, and all that road going, all the people

dreaming in the immensity of it, and in Iowa I know by now the children must be crying in the land where they let the children cry, and tonight the stars'll be out, and don't you know that God is Pooh Bear? the evening star must be drooping and shedding her sparkler dims on the prairie, which is just before the coming of complete night that blesses the earth, darkens all rivers, cups the peaks and folds the final shore in, and nobody, nobody knows what's going to happen to anybody besides the forlorn rags of growing old, I think of Dean Moriarty, I even think of Old Dean Moriarty the father we never found, I think of Dean Moriarty.

What did it mean? This wasn't America. This wasn't New Jersey. This was Canada. And if there was some important hidden message there, I wasn't getting it.

I also read the last page of The *Brothers Karamazov*, thinking this was also just some kind of game Marlene had tried to play on me. Without reading the whole book, I didn't understand who the players were or what was going on. Somebody had died, that's all I could figure out and a family had gathered together.

"And may the dead boy's memory live for ever!" Alyosha added again with feeling.

"For ever!" the boys chimed in again.

"Karamazov," cried Kolya, "can it be true what's taught us in religion, that we shall all rise again from the dead and shall live and see each other again, all,

Ilyusha too?"

"Certainly we shall all rise again, certainly we shall see each other and shall tell each other with joy and gladness all that has happened!" Alyosha answered, half laughing, half enthusiastic.

"Ah, how splendid it will be!" broke from Kolya.

"Well, now we will finish talking and go to his funeral dinner. Don't be put out at our eating pancakes —it's a very old custom and there's something nice in that!" laughed Alyosha. "Well, let us go! And now we go hand in hand."

"And always so, all our lives hand in hand! Hurrah for Karamazov!" Kolya cried once more rapturously, and once more the boys took up his exclamation: "Hurrah for Karamazov!"

41

Russell was in the middle of what he called "a really big deal" when it came time to drive me to the airport, so Chen drove me. She told me how much she liked having me staying there with them.

Pin came along and I felt bad I hadn't really given the kid a chance to get to know me better—the new me, anyway. He still seemed like a lonely kid. A kid who could have used an older brother.

"Maybe you can come visit me some day," I told him, knowing full well this was unlikely to happen.

"Maybe," he said. "I'd like that. You'd show me the Northwest Arm?"

"How'd you know about that?" I asked.

"Garrett told me," he answered. "He said you were very brave."

"I wasn't," I said.

And then it was time to fly home.

~

Canada is a really large country, spanning six time zones. The only country that has more time zones is Russia, I think.

As the Air Canada jet lifted into the clear blue sky, I let it sink in that I was leaving my brother behind. Possibly for good. That scared the hell out of me.

And I was pretty sure I'd never see Marlene again.

So two of the most important people to me in the world would not be around to guide me, comfort me or help me get through a single awful day—and I envisioned awful days ahead.

Going back home. Home to what?

I figured my mom needed me, of course. By now she'd know of Garrett's decision, and it would be tough on her. So I'd have to take up the slack. Garrett had always been better with Mom's problems than I was, but it looked like I'd have to figure out what to do.

As we flew over the Cascade Mountains, I tried to envision that cabin on Gabriola Island that they'd be living in—Garrett, Marlene and Jessica. Not exactly cut off from civilization, but rustic. An old house on the shores of the water facing east. Facing sunrise. Mountains in the distance on the mainland. Big trees, maybe, like those ones in Stanley Park.

We'd had a moment in Stanley Park, Garrett and me. In the midst of all the sadness and despair of hospital visits, we had made the long hike to the park and Garrett and I sat on a rock by the water with those giant trees behind us and he looked up at the clouds in the sky.

"It makes you think that somewhere, somehow, something really means something. Doesn't it?"

He said that. He really did. I didn't know why he said such a thing just then. At first, I didn't know what he meant.

Well, maybe I did. I mean, I could feel something. Something larger, something more important. But they were just clouds, right? A cloud is just a cloud, water suspended in the sky.

On the plane, looking down at the interior mountains of British Columbia, I did feel something like that. Those mountains were just big chunks of rock. They were just there. They didn't *mean* anything. But I felt something large. Just like in the park. I felt connected to them. Even though that didn't make any sense. But that made me feel better.

And as we flew east there were more mountains, and then vast flat empty prairies, then forests. I felt like maybe I should spend my life just wandering across this country. Or beyond.

But by the time we descended through the grey clouds to the airport in Toronto, where I had to change planes, I lost whatever reverie, whatever connection, I had felt.

In the jostling crowd of the airport, I felt disconnected and alone. I got lost. People were not helpful. No one cared. I ended up at the wrong terminal. I nearly missed my flight.

When I got on the plane—the last passenger to embark —the airline attendant told me that they had held up the flight just for me. Apparently, everyone on the plane knew the flight had been held up for me. I couldn't help but notice the avalanche of dirty looks as I clumped down the aisle and awkwardly threw my bag into the bin overhead.

I wanted to run off that plane right then. Turn myself around and go back to the West Coast. But I had no money for a flight. My father wouldn't want to shell out more travel money for the unwanted son. I was back to being Hopeless.

I fell into my seat, annoying the hell out of the two people already sitting in that aisle. The plane was full, but I felt more alone than I'd felt in my life.

I felt like shit.

~

My mom met me at the airport. I wasn't really expecting that.

"Your brother's not with you?"

"No," I said. "Didn't he tell you?"

She started to cry. "He did. I read his email and I called him. He said he was sorry, but he insisted that he was staying, but I didn't believe him."

"Did you try to talk him out of it?"

She stopped crying and tugged me to sit down on a bench with her. Someone from the plane walked by and gave me yet another dirty look. *The stupid kid who delayed the flight. Causing more grief, probably. Making that woman cry.*

"I didn't," she said. "I knew he needed something. Something I couldn't give him. I didn't want to hold him back. But I was sure he'd change his mind and come home with you."

She took out a handkerchief and blew her nose, then put her hand on my shoulder. "I guess now it's just you and me."

"It's good to be home," I lied, and gave my mom a big hug.

But home felt different. Even though Garrett had been a ghost in recent times, it felt weird not having him there. I wondered if we would hear from him. I wondered if they made it to the island okay. I wondered what it would be like for the three of them living together, taking care of Marlene, making the best of it for her until the end. And what would happen then?

The day after I arrived, Russell phoned my mom at work, asking if I made it home okay. Good old Dad. But he had not heard anything from Garrett. He said that he thought Garrett was acting irresponsibly. Mom said he was shocked that Garrett didn't want to stay in Vancouver with him.

The man was about as clueless as he could be. Hopeless, in his own way. Was I my father's son? Both of us with the stubborn gene. Set in our own ways.

It took me a couple of days to get up the courage to go back to school, and that's when Tasker lit into me. I wanted to tell him to shove it where the sun don't shine, but somehow he got to me.

Maybe it was partly because Marlene had got me reading those books she left. I had been reading *On the Road* on the plane to get my mind off the other passengers' dirty looks. I'd liked it a lot more than Dostoevsky, but I still found it baffling. It seemed to me that most of the characters were lost, searching for something but they didn't know what.

Yet reading it made wonder if anyone would care if I told *my* story. Not a novel. But the real story. I didn't think anyone would.

And then there I was back in school, getting berated by Tasker, telling him next to nothing as to why I'd been missing school. Being a stubborn asshole like I'd always been. And he made this outrageous plan for me to write 50,000 words about me. My story. He told me that if I did it, he'd convince Lombardo and the principal to let me pass and go on to the next grade.

I was pretty sure I couldn't do it. But I said yes to get him off my back.

I thought I'd write some bullshit thing that would really piss him off and that would be the end of it. But he gave me this old beat-up laptop (with no internet capability) and told me I could work in the library as long as I was civil. Yeah, that's the word he used. Civil.

In the library I could look at girls. Or I could read. Tasker wasn't there peering over my shoulder or anything. Sometimes I could just goof off and still no one would say a word about it.

But I got bored. Real bored. Real fast.

So I started writing.

And writing.

And it just kind of came floating out. The story I wanted to tell.

I watched the word count day by day and then one day, there it was.

And here it is.

Are you counting, Mr. Tasker? Are you surprised I did it?

Epilogue

Tasker read it and said it was good. "I counted 50,849," he added. "I only asked for 50,000."

"I got carried away."

"But that literary stuff—Kerouac and Dostoevsky—that was bullshit. You just threw that in 'cause you thought you could trick me into thinking you were some kind of intellectual kid."

And maybe I did. But I wrote about those books and some others from the famous pile because that was what Marlene kept telling me: that I needed to get out of my own head and read about different times, different people.

So I did what she told me.

~

Mom had been calling Russell from work to find out if he'd heard anything more from Garrett, but he kept saying that there had not been a single word. We didn't know what to think. Had they just disappeared into the West Coast wilderness?

And then one day a letter arrived.

A letter. Like in the mail, with the bills and the junk mail.

No return address. But postmarked Gabriola Island.

I ripped it open.

Dear Mom and Nick,

Sorry for the long wait. We're settled in now and making a go of it. Jessica, Marlene and I are here on the island. The cottage is old, very old. But it's okay. There's a retired doctor on the island who comes over to help us with Marlene sometimes. And a VON nurse. But most of the time it's just Jessica and me taking care of her.

It wasn't easy getting Marlene here. In fact, nothing has been easy.

But we're here. And we're staying here.

Jessica and I have become the best of friends. She really couldn't do this without help. Without me. I feel needed, really needed for maybe the first time in my life.

I know this was the right thing to do. I feel it in my bones.

Marlene is about the same as when you saw her, Nick. Tired a lot. But stable for now. But so much happier than being in the hospital. Still on pain meds but trying to cut back. The old doc stays on top of that and consults with the hospital back on the mainland.

Every day is a challenge. Jessica gives us both a pep talk when things get rough. I think I need it more than Marlene.

But the truth is, I love it here. I'm sorry I didn't

come home, Mom. I hope you'll understand. Do you think we all have a special place in the world where we need to be to be happy? I do. And I think I found it.

I don't want to bum you out, but we talk a lot about death, the three of us. Marlene's time is limited, but she is where she wants to be.

And so am I.

I'm going to do better at staying in touch. I want to hear what you are both up to. I miss you both. But I don't miss much else from back home.

I get up early each morning and walk down to the water. Everything is different here. I can't quite explain it. But different. The sea smells different. The trees are different. And that's what I needed too. Something different.

I don't know how I found my way here but I did. I expect things will get pretty bad eventually. For Marlene, I mean. But she is teaching me how to live. And so is Jessica. Something new each day. I guess we're like a weird little family. And I like that.

Love,

Garrett

It's warm now, almost summer. On a good day I get up early —real early, like five o'clock in the morning—and walk down to the Northwest Arm to watch the sun come up. It's the weirdest thing. The birds start chirping while it's still dark. Right before the first bit of light comes in from the east over the city. I usually walk down along the pebbly beach to watch the tiny waves lap on the shore and listen to those birds.

I think about Garrett, four time zones away. If it's clear out there, he'll see the sunrise four hours after me. And I wonder about his day. I miss him of course. But I have this good feeling inside knowing he's out in that cabin with Jessica and Marlene.

And then, if the skies are clear, the sun comes up and begins to sparkle on the water from the Atlantic. No ice on the water, of course.

And the birds get louder and louder, and I start to hear the sound of traffic on the streets behind me. And it's right about then that I remind myself that nothing is hopeless. Not even me.

end

About the author

Lesley Choyce is the author of several books of literary fiction, poetry, creative nonfiction and young adult novels. He teaches Creative Writing at Dalhousie University and his books have been published in Danish, German, Spanish, French, Swedish and Slovenian. He has won The Dartmouth Book Award, The Atlantic Poetry Prize and The  Ann Connor Brimer Award and has been short-listed for the Governor-General's Award.

He lives at Lawrencetown Beach, Nova Scotia, where he surfs year-round in the North Atlantic.